I0519670

Also by Rechan

Handcuffs & Lace
Will of the Alpha (editor)
Taboo (editor)
Will of the Alpha 2 (editor)
Will of the Alpha 3 (editor)
Dungeon Grind (co-editor)
Intimate Little Secrets
Feral! (editor)

In Flux

Edited by Rechan

In Flux

Production © Rechan and FurPlanet Productions

"Aesop's Universe: Savages in Space" © 2018 Bill Kieffer
"Wild Dog" © 2018 Franklin Leo
"Good Boy" © 2018 Friday Donnelly
"Never Lick a PVC Vixen" © 2018 Tarl "Voice" Hoch

Cover illustration by Sabretoothed Ermine
https://www.furaffinity.net/user/sabretoothedermine

Published by FurPlanet Productions
Dallas, TX
http://www.FurPlanet.com

Print ISBN 978-1-61450-453-5
Electronic ISBN 978-1-61450-454-2

First Edition Trade Paperback 2018

All rights reserved. No portion of this work may be reproduced in any form, in any medium, without the express permission of the author.

Table of Contents

Aesop's Universe: Savages in Space

Bill Kieffer

Thandiwe's naked, tawny body shifted, crouching down silently. A change in the wind dictated she move, the breeze lifting her Feline scent away from the herd of gazelle. The outliers obligingly wandered closer. She needed to pick a target she could fell with her limited supply of six arrows.

Of all the Lion hunters on the Bradbury, Thandiwe was the most adept with the bow and only passingly fair with the knife. Natural selection, her mother said, had given her useful hawk-like eyes. As a designated breeder/hunter for the new world, farsightedness was considered a blessing. Thandiwe would have preferred the eyes of an owl, so that she could read without squinting.

Above all the gods of the universe, the Colonists believed in Natural Selection. Gene-engineering might make a perfect hunter, but it would never make a perfect society. There would be things to hunt on virgin Veldt, even if they had to stock the world themselves. Elephants, deer, gazelle, bison, and hundreds of other saved "live-stock" in digital, frozen embryo state could be cloned over and over again until the ship ran out of power.

Therefore, choosing the weakest member was difficult, perhaps much harder than it would have been in a truly natural wild. There was more than meat and skin at stake in these hunting trips. The one elderly doe she'd chosen could be in the field in seven different locations in different incarnations. The task was to make the best possible choice from one's own observations. This not only thinned the herd properly, ensuring its survival, but also earned your respect from the council.

The arrow flew.

The doe's head turned at the string's release and its left eye socket swallowed the arrow almost whole. It stood still for a moment; its right hind leg twitching as if it alone of the four was trying to run away. The gazelle fell over with a spasm as another arrow clumsily bounced off the back of its head.

The herd broke and ran, causing Bobby to stand and whoop so as not to be trampled. That would be an embarrassing death for any Lion, even one of the Crew. Thandiwe met him at "their" kill. She watched him trot over and admired the civilized cut of mane that marked him as an outsider, the tight muscles under his supple, tawny hide, the blunt fingers, and smooth bulge of flesh barely hidden in his khaki tights.

She found his broken arrow and smiled as she tossed the pieces to him. Thank goodness the males of her tribe were not expected to hunt. He was so cute, staring at the broken arrowhead, realizing that the kill wasn't his to claim.

Well, at least he tried to hunt, Thandiwe gave him that.

"We should get this into refrigeration right away," Bobby announced, trying to take charge in the Crew way.

Thandiwe placed her head on the chest of the herbivore and, checking for a heartbeat, she thanked it for its giving of its life to them, for providing meat to their fire, and its hide for their clothing. "We have some time for that, my fisherboy. Hours yet. Why not enjoy the privacy we've been granted for a victory celebration?" She teased, "Unless you forgot that magic device?"

"Didn't forget, Beloved." Bobby smiled and closed his eyes in a blush of sorts. The Colonists needed to live as "primitively" as possible without causing resentment. Yet, they could not help but be aware of the wider "world" beyond the walls that held up the sky. He pulled out a small rectangular thing. "Medical device," he corrected.

Thandiwe smiled in return. For a young Huntress, she was a bit of a dreamer. It was Bobby's access to things like this medical device and condoms that had made him attractive. That and the fact that the Crewman seemed so much different than the other males in her village. Competent in his profession and yet willing to hunt with her. If they made it to the Promised Land safely…

…and if Veldt didn't need much tending…

…and if he chose to leave the ship and come live with her planetside…well, of course, he would need her something fierce. She liked that in a male.

They stepped closer. The device brushed against the downy golden fur on her stomach. Her fur stood on end an inch out on either side of her muscled hips. She nibbled his lips and ran a hand through a short and clean mane that only a crewman could maintain. Would maintain. The need for this man tightened her chest; moistened her loins.

"Wait," he laughed and pleaded. "This will take a minute. Less than a minute."

Their fur and his mane rippled with some minor static electricity that only she noticed. He was too busy staring into his magic tinder and flint box. "You are not close to your fertile period." His tail flicked wildly as he tried to make sense of the curious readings. "You must have just have your… what's wrong?"

She placed her fingers over his small, flatter muzzle. The biosphere was silent of birds and insects. The only sound she heard was his breathing and the oft forgotten background noises of the massive ship's mechanical parts.

Bobby knew these sounds better than she. Something was stressing something somewhere. His eyes darted for the nearest hidden lifepod, the whiff of fear radiating between the two them. They grabbed each other's hand, Bobby pulling.

Before she could ask him what was wrong, the air squeezed her ankles and swept the words from her mouth. The ground threw her up with a great geyser of dirt and steel. Their kill fell into the hole and spit out aflame a second later. Bobby grabbed her out of the air. His short pants instantly shaped into a unitard around him. His life belt activated in the same second, covering him in a thin nimbus of safety. This he placed between Thandiwe and the geyser of super-heated gasses as he ran.

Thandiwe passed out before the heat fully carbonized the meat of her legs.

***

From Robert Lion-612's report:

The Hunting Dome was compromised in two areas. Passenger Thandiwe and I were in the area adjacent environmental processing and reclamation when the sudden gravimetric shift from the unidentified incursion event caused engine nacelle 14 to shear off from the Bradbury, and cause ruptures in the condenser coils under the platform, which was known to be vulnerable due to metal fatigue.

My life belt performed beyond its expected perimeters, allowing me to save Passenger Thandiwe, but not without life threatening injuries. Despite getting her safely ensconced into lifepod H-150, the pod failed to cycle the super-heated air out before her right lung collapsed. Her face and limbs were severely burnt. I used an entire med kit to keep as much of her as alive as possible. The Launch button sputtered and popped the entire time. I heard the clamps opening and closing. I was unable attempt to re-enter the damaged dome, as the pod door did not know what to do with the mixed signals it was getting.

The computer could not confirm that the lifepod would stay obediently at its bay. I fought to keep the pod from launching with one or more clamps still engaged until the lifebelt failed to protect me from the remaining ambient heat and lingering coolant gases. The lifepod sustained damage and needs to be rebuilt or replaced, assuming the council approves. It will not survive planetfall.

The remaining Passengers in the Dome were in the opposite side of the biosphere. They escaped initial injury from the superheated gasses due to their placement. *I was alerted when they reached a lifepod of their own. The door to that lifepod failed to close when the outer shell of the deck gave way and allowed the atmosphere to leave via explosive decompression.*

It should be noted, my records indicate the Passengers attempted to seal lifepod H-152 for more than five minutes before the fatal event.

Unit 152 also needs to be replaced or discarded as the council sees fit. It will not survive launch.

I have three recommendations.

We need to change emergency drills so that the passengers learn when they need to choose another lifepod. This is a resource effective solution.

We should not return the bodies to their families. Considering their superstitions, we should tell the families that the bodies were blown into space. Additionally, we should not weaken their trust in our technology and guidance; especially in the final years of our flight.

Passenger Thandiwe would benefit from a full healing tank immersion. I have a full and complete DNA scan of her healthy body. In addition to being personally attached to Thandiwe myself, I would like to point out that the Bradbury Council could use a "win" in light of the recent tragedy.

***

Thandiwe opened her eyes, surprised to find that she had eyelids to open. She'd awoken to near darkness. There were dozens of small bright lights in the room. Little crew lights. Tell-tales, Bobby would have called them. A harsh sterile smell permeated the air.

Obviously, this was not the Lion Village Deck. From that, Thandiwe deduced that she'd been injured enough to require Crew assistance. She'd been with Bobby. He'd been protected by his devices. Beyond that, recall balked. If she had survived, logic dictated that he had also.

Not blind, at least.

The Lioness counted her limbs without moving her head. They were numb, but seemed whole. Soft tubes entered her body in weird places. Thandiwe passed out twice, probing the areas where actual pain and the memory of pain became confused. The urge to tear out the wires and to stalk the corridors as if she were in enemy territory, came and went. Healing and rest were needed; one would beget the other.

"You are awake." The room announced softly in the Southern Heartland tongue she had grown up speaking. Female voice. "It is night cycle on your native deck. You have awakened thrice for an extended period of time. Do you recall those events?"

"Not really," the Huntress answered. Her weak voice frightened her. It did not sound like her at all. The air had turned to fire and then ice; she supposed that having any voice at all was a godsend.

"Your voice is improving," the room sounded pleased. "We removed the tracheal tube on your last conscious period. What is your current pain level from 1 to 10, ten being the worst pain you have ever felt?"

Thandiwe remembered being burned alive. That would have to be the worst pain ever, but it had been so short. Barely more than an instant before blackness claimed her. "Seven?" she asked the room as if it were a better judge of these things.

"I have alerted the doctor and your family."

"What about Bobby?"

The room hummed with wise humor. There was a soft beep from one of the devices near her arm. Thandiwe felt a strange warmth, and vaguely wondered if she had peed on her own arm somehow. "Robert Lion-612 has a steady feed of your biomedic readings. Were he awake, I'm sure he'd have been here for the extubation."

Extubation? It sounded like a coming of age rite. The warmth spread through her and the Lioness thought about Bobby's penis. The golden sheath rolling down and the pale pinkness of it. The boys in the village, they had fiery red members with a cluster of white bumps at the base. Spikes, they called them, but the bumps seemed little more than short bristles. Young males were too ready to show off, as if their poke sticks were all they had to offer the best warrior of the village deck.

Thandiwe wanted none of that. She'd had Bobby in her twice before. She loved the smoothness and the slickness of him, but hated the membrane he used to cover his shaft. "To prevent unwanted complications," the crewman apologized each time.

Pregnancies, he meant. She knew the rules, but the flesh yearned for more.

The spreading warmth swallowed conscious thought as it reached her ears and her mouth. The hospital room and its sterile smells vanished into a dream of amber plains and a wind that tickled her nose with the smell of her lover.

***

Thandiwe awoke to find Bobby sitting at her bedside, in his full crew uniform. The brown jumpsuit with black piping and glyphs that meant nothing to her looked crisp and impossibly clean. His mane was cut even more severely than the day of the nightmare. He watched her looking at him as if they were estranged friends meeting at a wake for a mutual friend. Her heart went out to him, even as her body reminded her that it was still healing.

"What happened?" she asked, disappointed at the formality in the Lion's bearing.

A careful smile followed a sigh, leaving only a trace of the heaviness in his eyes. "Some large FTL tried jumping ahead, past the debris field. The gravimetric wake fouled our own systems and caused an inertia compensator to blow. One of the FTL engines was sheered off its mooring and scraped up the outer hull."

Thandiwe understood enough of what he had said, but it hadn't been what she'd meant to ask. It was typical Bobby to avoid awkward feelings. "Are we okay?"

"The ship is fine," he said, madly misconstruing Thandiwe's

questions again. No matter, the huntress was used to running down prey. Despite low reserves, the Lioness knew she could still outlast Bobby, so let him babble. "It's not like we need the FTL systems from here, so having less mass means braking will be easier when we reach Veldt. We lost a lot of coolant and water though, and we need that. The other ship, they probably got hit harder than us. They came out of hyperspace two AU in front of us with their ram scoop open...they look dead... but... everyone's on edge."

"Bobby," Thandiwe said firmly, despite her throat advising otherwise. "How are we? Me and you. I can see your face and you're... I don't know. My Beloved... are you mad at me for inviting you to hunt?"

Bobby's eyes went wide and he practically leapt to her side. Tender thick fingers stroked her face. "No, no," he reassured her. "It's just that the last time I saw you, you were..." He asked the room something in Crew and the room filled in his missing words in her tongue: Carrion Feast. "I... I was afraid that you'd be mad at me for not saving you."

"Since when is it the male's job to save the hunter? But you did save me, Bobby, you did. And my pain is only a three now."

Room thanked her.

She tried to take Bobby's hand, to reassure him in return. Nothing happened, but the muffled sounds of fabric being pulled on. Numb limbs whispered a sensation of some sort.

"You're restrained until the nerves fully grow back or we get all these tubes out of you." Bobby said, running his hands down her left arm. Most of her responded to the touch but little came from beyond her wrist, except that the fingers felt large and fat, as if she'd been stung. "You were hurt very, very badly. You might have to relearn to..." He swallowed his words. "Anyway... you're very lucky. We lost people in the accident." He stressed the word accident, as if he were in the habit of reassuring her that it was an accident.

No, not her, she decided. Other people. Future colonists and possibly other crew.

Thandiwe was a huntress; a warrior. "They think it might have been an attack?"

Bobby smiled, embarrassed. "Who can rule that out? Other seeded planets had hundreds of years of development behind them. Veldt would be valuable real estate for any culture ready to launch a colonist ship. The other ship is still on the path to our 'Promised Land.' If they get there first, they'd have a better claim. More likely they don't even know we exist. We will catch up with them in a few months as we brake… or even a few weeks if their maneuvering thrusters don't come on. Their passage out of hyperspace set a thousand micro-corrections into motion. We can't watch them the way the war hawks would like." Bobby seemed to be relieved to get that off his chest. "But I don't want you to worry about that."

Thandiwe smiled, such concerns seemed a million miles away. "Is the room still drugging me?"

Room answered yes, even as Bobby tried to explain that her treatment still wasn't complete. "I don't mind. I dreamed you were inside of me. Warming me, healing me, licking me… will you do that for me?" She floated on a cloud. Bobby, embarrassed, seemed to say something, but his words were so far away. Already, Thandiwe was dreaming of hidden folds of flesh blossoming as her fisherboy exploded within her, sending soothing ripples through her body. Those ripples rocked her to sleep even has Bobby's wordless voice droned on in a warmed lullaby.

***

When Thandiwe woke up again, Bobby was back in civilian clothing. He smiled at her and she smiled back. "I feel excellent," she told him and the room before either of them could ask. She paused, testing the restraints. "But my voice still sounds off… and I am still restrained. Do I really have more healing to do?"

"A Crisis Counselor has been assigned and will here shortly," Room told her. The Lioness looked curiously at her crewman. These were two words that she understood, just not put together in that way.

"Do you remember when I told you yesterday that we lost people?" Bobby put a golden hand on her shoulder, stroking fresh, baby-soft fur. Maybe it was the angle or the numbness, but, his hand seemed smaller than before. "We lost all the other Lions on the Hunting Deck. And a great deal of the livestock."

Thandiwe knew the other hunters well. They were her sisters in spirit, if not in blood. They'd wandered in deeper so as to give Bobby and Thandiwe some alone time. Six Lionesses that would never see Veldt. The potential genetic diversity would be impacted, she realized, as an afterthought.

I was lucky to have survived. Had Thandiwe been with anyone but a crewman, they'd have slashed her throat in the lifepod as a mercy; to join the hunt anew with ancestors.

Thandiwe sighed and tried to console her poor male. She was still restrained. She stamped out the urge to struggle.

Crew were notoriously skittish about heavy emotional displays, she thought, making the connection to what a crisis counselor must be. "There's always risk when hunting. Even in a controlled environment like a Hunting Deck. I will miss and mourn my friends, of course. I do not need to speak with your shaman."

"Protocol," Bobby said in equal parts of discomfort, assurance, and concern. "Besides, you were injured very badly. We had to employ ship-science to heal you."

Thandiwe looked about the room, dramatically. "I have not been drugged to the point where I did not notice the very walls were speaking to me."

As Bobby opened his mouth to speak, Thandi realized how much sharper her vision was. She gasped as her tongue probed her teeth in a quick count. There were no gaps. No cracked teeth from an antelope that hadn't been quite ready to die. All her teeth were smooth and painfree!

"You got them to gene-engineer me?" A spike of happiness

rushed through her, despite the horrified look on his face.

"No," Bobby said, stroking her cheek. "No. We don't have the tampers to spare… they are too precious. Not even to save a breeding colonist." He blinked and seemed to consider his next words very carefully. "But we were able to use the Vat to reconstruct you… to heal you by rebuilding your body based on your genes. You know how genes work, right?"

Thandiwe nodded, not at all insulted. She was an avid book reader. Much of her tribe would not care to know such things. It wasn't as important as weapons, traps, and fighting skills. "Blueprints," she said, using the Crew word.

"So, your body was re-built as intended."

"You cloned my body?"

"No, we tricked your body into regenerating itself. Your spine was untouched, Thandi, but your limbs and a lot of your organs are only a few weeks old. Your eyes had to be regrown." At her fallen expression, he steered her face gently to meet his eyes. "You are what nature's blueprints meant for you to be. We just added water and lots of proteins."

Thandiwe nodded, understanding the gist. Still, there was a weight in his eyes. There was something he could not say. "Okay, if the gods meant my eyes to be good, why did they go bad?"

Bobby, relieved again that she had asked about her eyes. "Something happened while you were developing either as a fetus or a little girl. Some virus, bug, or even some a vitamin deficiency that your shaman missed."

Thandiwe suddenly felt trapped, tied down like this. The warrior in her demanded escape. "Where's my mother? My family? You said we lost people." The huntress hated that she sounded even a little frightened.

"Your family is fine." Bobby squeezed her numb left hand. She was sure she squeezed back. "They just find the medicinal smell and the blinking lights to be very upsetting. Plus, they had a very hard time seeing you like this." Bobby looked away and seemed to speak to her numb hand. "They mourned you like you were dead the whole time you were in the Vat, healing."

"When we marry, they will really mourn," Thandiwe said to lighten the mood. She was surprised to see Bobby's eyes tear. Males were so emotional, but these did not seem to be happy tears.

Before the Lioness could respond, a female crewman let herself into the room. Thandiwe saw that she was some sort of Feline with black stripes on her orange cheeks and white fuzzy chin. She wore almost the same brown uniform as Bobby often did, only with red and white piping.

"Lieutenant?" she asked Bobby in Crew with a quick glance at Thandiwe for an introduction. "I'm Dr. Jane. Is he ready for me, yet?"

Thandiwe blinked, translating and re-translating the doctor's words in her mind.

He.

Thandiwe understood suddenly all too well why she'd been restrained once she was out of her healing coma. Ship's science had turned her male. They hadn't wanted her to touch herself until they thought her ready to discover this. She roared with rage and betrayal, insane at hearing the deep bellow tear itself from her throat.

Damn them all for saving her and condemning her to hell in an alien body! Bobby threw calming words at her, but she no longer cared about Crew sensitivity. It was more than the proud huntress could stand, being betrayed like this.

"You, get out!" Dr. Jane ordered Bobby to leave the room. At his hesitation, the orange shaman bellowed, "That's an order!"

Bobby fled, which helped. The needed healing tears came once her suitor was gone. She simply could not cry like a little boy in front of her suitor.

Only, was he still her suitor?

Dr. Jane sat on the edge of the bed and spoke a few soft words to remind Thandiwe that she was here when she was ready to talk.

***

Thandiwe stared at her penis. It seemed to roll on its own accord. She was repulsed to feel these sensations. How did Bobby ever get any of his important work done? He recommended tight cup briefs during one of his now rare visits.

Dr. Jane touched the penis in a very clinical manner, without asking. Thandiwe, after all, wasn't about to touch it. "You're well enough that you no longer need a catheter," the doctor chided. "You must care for yourself, especially since you are being returned to your deck."

"I don't want this thing. I want it off of me." Her voice had grown deeper as her body went thicker.

"Now Thandiwe," Dr. Jane said as she simply pulled down the sheath and swabbed the thick red member with a sterilized cleaner.

Thandiwe gasped as the thing was no longer the numb roll of flesh it had been a few days ago. The Lioness knocked the Tiger's hand away from her maleness.

Dr. Jane barely paused except to meet Thandiwe's eyes in challenge. "We discussed this. This is your genetic code. Androgen insensitivity syndrome is rare, but not unknown. Our only recourse under normal ship conditions would be surgical. Gender confirmation surgery would *not* make you a viable reproductive colonist. This form can make babies. So, you're going to stay male and service any and all females you can poke your penis into."

Dr. Jane finished cleaning the strange member between them. "Now," she said, annoyed, "Do you need me to wipe your ass, too?"

Thandiwe glared at the smaller Feline. "No," she said bitterly. "That part hasn't changed much."

That was not quite true. As a male, her tail was thicker and her anus seemed to ride up with it, above her butt cheeks. Her tawny balls and penis couldn't decide if they wanted to ride behind her under her tail or in front of her, where Bobby's package had always rested, sitting or standing.

"Why isn't my...*stuff* the same as Bobby's?" she asked. "I have those stupid spikes and my penis looks all angry and red. Plus... Bobby's has a head on his."

Dr. Jane had to break off her anger before she could answer. "Crew is genetically altered to be more... interchangeable. So, even though Bobby's a Lion, he could have sex with most of the Species on-board. As Crew, the more homogeneity, the better." Dr. Jane smiled, a shadow of embarrassment. "Not that we all have to have sex with each other. Now, your people, the Lion and the other Colonial species—you are what we will all revert into after a few generations without gene-engineering. You are all the results of natural selection. The only thing we alter is a small portion of the brain that keeps everyone straight during development."

"Straight?"

"When any shaman does a prenatal, he gives the mother a drug that... Have you read anything about the hypothalamus or the amygdala? Inter-hemispheric neural connectivity?" Dr. Jane waved her hand dismissively, catching the blank look on the Huntress' face. "We make you all breeders from birth."

"What else is there?" Thandiwe was at least distracted from thinking about the meat between her legs. This seemed one of the secret things Crew hid from the Colonists. She was riveted.

For her part, Dr. Jane seemed to realize that the Bradbury was near the end of its travels. Soon, none of this would matter. "Oh, there are a variety. Girls who like girls. Boys who like boys. Boys that want to be treated like girls. Which is why you shouldn't push Robert away. He's a boy that likes everyone."

Thandiwe looked at Dr. Jane, appalled.

"I don't mean to say that he's a slut or anything. He loves you... Rók'e or no Rók'e."

Thandiwe was very confused. "Didn't you make me... a Breeder?"

"Well, we thought we did, but sexuality is a complex thing, even with all our science. If a young passenger displays non-productive tendencies, the shaman is supposed to slip the kid some special candy and suddenly the opposite sex starts looking good to them." Dr. Jane looked Thandi in the eyes and shrugged. "Obviously, your interest in Bobby convinced your shaman that you were a breeder. I could give that candy to you now, but here's the thing, you love him," Dr. Jane said seriously, "I wouldn't be a party to any decision that changed that. Provided that you were willing to become a sperm donor, you'll never have to stick your 'thing' anywhere you do not want it to go."

Shocked and a little confused, Thandiwe agreed with a short nod of her head.

***

Thandiwe itched everywhere. The nerves had regrown everywhere but her fingertips. It was an effort not to scratch herself, especially in the crotch with its willful flesh. The male body fur was thicker than she was used to and the mane was the worst of it. Dr. Jane refused to trim it for her.

"The males in your culture do not cut their headfur. You can keep combing it or grow dreadlocks," Dr. Jane said firmly. "Or invent shears."

She would have also preferred to keep her scars, for she had earned every one of them.

I will just have to earn new ones, the Lioness decided.

"I've queued the time lapse video of healing," the Tiger told her just before she left to make her rounds. "Just tell the room when you are ready to view it."

Young Thandiwe had been exposed to small and short videos during her school days. Ship Safety Instructions. Zoo Habitats that offered student exchanges. First Aid demonstrations. Images that feed information into hungry minds. It was all proof that "magic" existed between all decks, and that those in the corridors between were not gods… and yet… and yet… She had never imagined that there would be one with her in it.

She did not recognize the pile of blackened skin and red meat as herself for the first few minutes. Her face was gone, replaced by a mask of plastic and metal. At three times the normal speed, medical Crew buzzed around the salvaged corpse they wouldn't let die. Then the vat was there, and the thing was there, inside of it, a body hanging by its head. Ten days swipe-jumped and the skin was peeled away, limbs cut away, until there was nothing to her but a skull and hips, with a spine and ribcage betwixt. The vat turned red with blood and Room explained that they'd almost lost her then.

At five times the normal speed, the ruined liquid was replaced with clear and techs surrounded her like busy bees in lab coats. Then her organs vanished one by one, to be replaced with the generic, gene-neutral replacements as they failed. Gene therapy would make them hers. This is where her body got past the damage that had made her female, Room explained on her third viewing. "Gene-neutral, the new organs expedited regrowth and did not block the uptake testosterone in your new tissues."

This explanation always confounded her. She did not understand testosterone or how she could have it in her body, yet not have it absorbed by her body, like some sort of curse or destiny that she had somehow barely escaped. All she really understood was that the artificial organs they gave her allowed this curse into her body.

This curse; this weakness.

This maleness.

The video sped forward at Thandi's command. New skin appeared as a thin translucent layer on the thing in the tank. At twenty times the speed, she almost missed her family's first visit. At normal speed, it was a jumpy collection of horrified expressions. Nothing, Thandiwe knew, had prepared her parents to see this monstrosity as their child.

The Lioness had a similar issue. Bobby had downplayed their initial reaction, which included her mother slamming a chair into the glass tube that held her healing body. *Blinking lights my ass*, she thought.

The video jumped ahead three days after that and for a moment she thought her mother must have damaged the healing Vat enough that they had to put her body in another. It was just a new angle. At a hundred times normal speed, the limbs began to regrow even as fur started to sprout. She saw her father make three flash speed visits during this time. The recording was rolled back and reviewed on almost normal speed. Each visit, his eyes were always rooted to her healing body. He was too primitive to even think to look at the camera and send a message to the future Thandiwe. Reassurances that she so terribly needed at the moment.

The video than focused on her face, the eyes growing back under the loose folds, the pink triangle nostrils expanding over the white and blue tubes going into her mouth. It was disturbing to see her own face outside of a mirror.

Mirrors had been rare in her village, but until Dr. Jane had decided that she was ready, they'd been totally absent from the healing room. Thandiwe chided her new male vanity, but she hadn't been able to do anything but stare at her reflection now that the Crew Shaman had allowed her this. She grew pleased to see the strongest looking male she'd ever seen looking back at her. Not an ounce of fat on that fierce visage, for Thandiwe's lifetime of exercise and hunting still had a say in how her body had regrown. The mane seemed silly on her face and it looked even sillier floating in the liquid around her unconscious face.

So much of Thandiwe's face still looked like the Huntress she still thought of herself as. Her skull hadn't changed its shape. The cheeks were slightly wider because her mouth and neck muscles were at least 50% thicker, but the lush brown mane hid it.

The video cut again to show what could barely be described as a right arm, it was a mere stump at first. In moments, it twitched rapidly before sprouting a long golden limb. This was less disturbing than her face had been. And then her legs. These did not bother her. They didn't even look like her legs. Her fingers and feet were now larger and thicker than they seemed in the video. These had developed to male standards in the Vat, but the muscle tone had been courtesy of a barely remembered electro stimulation that encouraged slow growing nerves to grow faster to catch up with her meat and skin.

As if the thought of meat had summoned it, the blossoming of her maleness filled the screen on the wall. It was hard for Thandiwe to watch this at first, but she replayed it over and over again. Dr. Jane and Bobby had explained that little button of flesh at the top of a woman's gonda was the same as a penis, but she thought they had meant it allegorically. It was something else entirely to see it sprout from a button to a lump and then a stick. The smooth slash between her legs healed up to a pinpoint and merged with the growing worm between her legs. Her chommie grew thick and loose until she saw hints of what would become her testicles.

With a great effort of will, Thandiwe held her vomit down. It wasn't as if she hadn't known where this was heading. A part of her had expected to see something magical. Instead, the recordings felt like a nature film for farmer boys.

She watched the video a total of five times at various speeds before she allowed herself to cry with Room locking the door to the outside world.

The worst of all that had happened was that Mother had only come to see me once, Thandiwe realized, drifting off to sleep. *Just that once, and maybe she had tried to kill her only daughter. Her only child.*

The Lioness asked the darkness, "Have my parents scheduled a visit yet?" The room responded with a bland negative, as if it realized that she was close to falling asleep.

They've avoided me for more than a month. That's long enough.

Feeling brave and a little angry, Thandiwe called out, "Can I have a full pass between here and my part of the ship for tomorrow?" Her voice broke like a male in puberty, but she was a bit too spent to care.

Room gave her a happy ping and updated her travel rating.

***

Thandiwe had never entered the Heartland decks from the crew levels before. Previous trips from her Tribe's deck have been either to the Hunting Grounds, the Zoo, or the School. At the time, these had appeared to be whole and separate worlds with a reality of their own. Yet, now she understood how small those sections had truly been. And how fragile.

Her path from the medical bay had taken her through a variety of sections; all designed to be universal and interchangeable at the mechanical level yet unique at the visceral level. Bobby had explained that Crew needed variety to function. A change of scenery was essential to keeping the technicians sane. Thandi had thought she had understood at the time, but having spent many weeks in a medical suite, she knew what it was like to starve for color, for variety. She drank in every little detail. There was every likelihood Passenger Thandiwe would never be allowed to come this way again. The Lioness suspected it was fear that slowed her step.

I am dawdling. These are but painted walls and these are not my home.

She pressed on past doors with icons of other sections of the Ark. Two miles and many decks later, the icons began to represent other species of Heartland. Eventually, the airlock with the Tribe's symbol appeared.

Thandiwe sat on the floor to rest her new legs and to examine the door. Gloss beige with a wheel in the middle seemed so anti-climatic. The plainness of it was disappointing.

The gate between worlds should evoke some sort of drama, she thought and then, on the heels of that, grunted. *Poetic nonsense. Damned testosterone is softening my mind.*

Thandiwe stood up, cutting her rest short, and waved her right hand over the keypad.

"Scanning for Contraband," the wall announced as her mirror image appeared before her. Room had offered her only two sets of clothing. A bold and obnoxious golden Dashiki made of something it called mudcloth or a brown unisex crew jumpsuit. Aware that Bobby's suit had saved them both, she selected the jumpsuit. The bulges in the magic mirror before her made her regret that choice. She was far too lean and muscular to be a male, yet, the wild mane and long, untrimmed tail tuft said she was no normal Lioness. Not to mention, *that* bulge, up-front and just below center mass.

Thandiwe wished the scan would find some unexpected issue that would send her back to Room where she would be safe. Safe, for a while, at least. Pride held her firm.

The scan pinged with a satisfaction that reminded her of Room's noises but when it spoke, it was with a strange male voice in Crew. "Please step inside the chamber. The other end will open when the area is clear of aboriginal observers. Estimated cycle will be thirty seconds." The door then opened outwardly and revealed the true gateway to her habitat.

Inside the airlock, the chamber looked a bit like a dark cavern made of stone. Thandiwe stepped inside, now aware of the bare pads on her feet. She'd never had a chance to really develop callouses and the gritty floor of the "cave" stung her feet. She hadn't thought to ask for sandals and Room hadn't suggested them. She forced herself not to act like a prissy Cat with wet feet. She was a warrior. The Lioness would have to put up with the pain.

The door closed behind her, Scanner detecting no one else at the entryway. There was a sense of movement as the embarkation chamber aligned with the habitat cell. Thandiwe had always known that her "world" was but a room in a berry on a twig of a bush full of such berries. Since the accident and her time in the Vat, her education of all things Bradbury had increased in leaps and bounds. Now she understood, if imperfectly, that the hectares that made up her village and the hunter grounds were but a cell in a structure that looked like a giant steel mulberry hanging on the tree that was the Bradbury. If the Bradbury was damaged beyond repair, the mulberry could drop and continue the long journey on its own, like the seed it was always meant to be.

Conversely, if her world had been damaged and threatened the well-being of the Bradbury and the other habitats, it could be released and destroyed. That little tidbit had kept the Lioness up for a few nights since discovering how fragile her world… all the little worlds of the Bradbury, really… were. In the ship's long journey, it only had happened once, Bobby confided in her. The details were "classified," a level of secrets the Crew treated with superstitious awe.

In a moment, the cave bounced ever so slightly and a breeze wandered into the cave as the door opened again behind her. Instead of the Bradbury's plain and narrow corridor, an arch of rocks and lush, verdant bush greeted her. The illusion of "fresh air" tickled her nose and for the first time, Thandiwe realized how much thicker her whiskers were like this.

She stepped out into the jungle, awed to feel as if she were really on a different world and not just inside a bubble of steel. Of course, she'd never been on a planet. She never knew what real gravity felt like. She was born and raised here, as were her parents and all her ancestors beyond memory. It was enough that it was not a part of the world of Crew.

The dirt and pebbles pressing into her delicate footpads distracted her from the feel of her bound genitals briefly. After a few steps, she looked back at the cave mouth and realized with a jolt where she was.

This was the cave that was closest to the taro fields, where some of the men of her village farmed.

There were not that many caves in her little world, after all. She had played in them all; half-heartedly searching for entry into the mysterious world of the Bradbury. Unlike the lifepods and the Deckways, the airlocks were hidden from the Villagers. Malcontents were not encouraged to escape into the Bradbury. The illusion of unlimited space was hard to maintain, yet important to the mental health of the Lions, or so Bobby had said.

The taro farm was closest, and was on the way to her hut, but her father would not be there. It was her father she needed to speak to first. Jito was kind-hearted and she did not fear his rejection. Even if he was repulsed by her new form, Thandiwe knew she could win him over in a very short time.

I am your child. Your only child.

It had always worked before.

She read the sky and confirmed the time of day. She had picked a good time. Her father would be in one of the herbal gardens, gathering fresh spices at his father's behest. Her mother would be checking traps along the river or teaching at the school on the far side of the disk. Assuming their routines hadn't changed. Their little world was slowing expanding its "day" to match the length of Veldt's rotation. All the little worlds clinging to the Bradbury were. Only the Crew kept their own cycles.

The new world was not meant for them.

Once out of the forest, the wind blew through her bushy mane, bringing with it a thousand scents that spoke of home. For the first time in a long time, Thandiwe stopped feeling sorry for herself.

Instead, she felt sorry for the Crew. They would die in their steel boxes, never knowing what a real world was supposed to be like.

***

The men at the herb gardens must have known who Thandiwe was, but they treated her as a stranger.

None of them could meet her eyes for long, most of them stared at her bulging crotch for far longer. They spoke to her as if she was Crew. They were, except for the staring, carefully and neutrally polite. Thandiwe found that somewhat exasperating, but at least she was able to ask after her father. There was only a few seconds of a blank stare before she was directed to the shrub gardens. She thanked them formerly and left, feeling all their eyes upon her. She tried not to think about the portent of those looks.

As a child, she'd been to the grove to help her father pick

berries; but it was only memories of stories told to her about her that Thandiwe could recall. Still, she passed the deckway to the grove many times and found it easily. Hidden within a baobab, the door parted at her touch. Like the airlock, this one scanned her and permitted access verbally. Which was odd, for none of the Lion deckways had spoken to her before.

Before. When I belonged here.

She paused and trembled, realizing that the ship functions saw her as Crew, not Colonist.

The Lioness stood in the gray and green corridor between the decks and leaned back against the sealed door. Thandiwe let herself cry. Huge racking sobs shook her body. Her awareness that her breasts no longer bounced when she cried like this made it worse. Even her head felt so tiny in her now huge hands. Everything about her was wrong. So very wrong!

I might get used to being male. I might somehow still have Bobby. My family might even accept me... someday. The Lioness tried to center herself on these thoughts, but the idea that she might count as Crew now and forever unsettled her so completely that even thinking her anonymous, sperm donated children might know landfall instead of her was simply too much.

In a few moments Scanner asked if she was in need of assistance. Thandiwe was tempted to call for the Crew Shaman, but a Huntress did not cry out for assistance for mere bad moods or unhappiness. Her own people would or would not accept her. She could not become a Colonist otherwise. The facts were as simple and as cruel as that. She had to win over Jito. Together, they could face her mother. With the teacher behind her, the village would have to accept Thandiwe transformed.

The Lioness picked herself up, wishing that she was as fine as her reassurances to Scanner. There would be time enough for tears for later. Her tail took a bit longer to settle down, and every sway of it pulled on the alien flesh between her legs.

No wonder males can only think of one thing at a time. These mad balls are awfully distracting.

Once in the Groves, she was subjected again to the strange aloofness of the male villagers. As they directed her to where her father was working, the Lioness found herself trying to distance herself from them. Their clothing varied in color and weave, none as fancy as the Room's idea of what was "native" wear. It occurred to her that Room must have provided an option from the first days of the Bradbury. Fashion obviously had drifted over the years.

No, she chided herself. *Fashion evolved.*

Then: *No, Fashion devolved; becoming more primitive.*

She would have to ask Bobby. Some crewman would have kept a history of such things.

Thinking about these trivialities kept her from thinking too much.

It took much too long to find her father. When Thandiwe did find him, Jito was alone, working calmly on a small row of bushes that seemed to hold on the rows and columns of wire framework. The air here was full of fuzzy yellow and black bees, as the flowers of the row were all in bloom. Her father glanced up, smiling briefly but vaguely as Thandiwe came within a yard or two of him. He seemed distracted and only mildly concerned, which the huntress took as a good sign.

"I'm so glad you're here," her father said in Crew, and then walked down the row, giving a "follow me" gesture without making further eye contact.

Thandiwe followed, curious. Her father squatted at the end of the row where the flowers had been mostly replaced by small berries. "I want to show you something." He fingered a young plant, recently transplanted from the nursery bed if she was correctly judging from the upturned soil. A single five-pointed flower had just begun to wilt, but there were a few black berries about a centimeter wide. "I hope you bought your sample tester. This is supposed to be solanum retro-flexum, but the hairs on the stem seem a little too prickly. I think the bees may have accidentally cross-pollinated this with a toxic night-shade variety."

Thandiwe was struck so speechless, even her ears seemed to fail her as he prattled on about the alkaloids of the wonderberry and the merits of maybe preserving this corrupted line…

"Father," Thandiwe managed as fear begin to bite, making her voice sound like some strange and annoyed male. The rebuilt throat sounded insane.

Jito looked up, puzzled. Their eyes met and held, but it was almost as if he could not see her.

"Father," she said, trying to soften her voice. "It's me, it's Thandi—"

As she spoke, the transformation in her father was almost as frightening as her own. Jito's eyes went wide and his fur rose up, so that even his graying mane seemed to stand on end. The older male's mouth opened in a silent roar of horror. He tried to scramble away, a crab running away from a boiling cauldron of water.

"You should not be here!" He shouted in his undignified retreat.

Thandiwe stood in place, rooted by her own horror as she watched the older male put the wire row of greenery between them. It would have been comic if her heart wasn't breaking.

Jito looked about in a panic, as if looking for help. Or witnesses. He saw none and seemed to catch his breath.

As if the wire row between them gave him strength and protection, her father stood. He raked his hands through his mane, but there was no pulling the shame and guilt from his face. "Your mother," Jito began, and then took a moment to regather himself anew. When he spoke again, it was in his native Southern Heartland. "Your mother had me cut a hole in the wall of your room. We carried your clothes and weapons out that hole and brought them to the graveyard with the remains of the others who died on the Hunting Grounds. Your mother scattered thorns behind us as we sung of your mighty deeds. You are dead to us."

"But," she cried, disbelief coloring her voice, "I'm not dead."

"What is death in this charade of life, Thandiwe?" He spat. "You belong to the Ship, now."

***

"It's all a spoiled charade."

Under a cracked and frozen sky, Thandiwe sat on a large rock and smeared the healing balm over the ruined pads of her feet. Bobby had brought it for her; leaving his station to rush to dry her tears on the Hunting Deck where she had almost died. Or had died, as far as her parents were concerned. To her people, death had never been the end of one's life. There was neither hell to fear nor heaven to look forward to. Just another world to wake up in. She hadn't expected that basic belief to be her undoing.

Her father's rejection had stunned her. He was emotional; she thought she could have won him over in time.

However, finding a line of thorns in the sand in front of the deckway to the Hunting Deck, was like a knife in her heart. Thandiwe had cried in the airlock between the decks again. Only this time, she cried all her tears. The thorns in front of Hunting door meant that her mother was sending her as a clear message as the video recording of her trying to destroy the Vat. That her daughter was truly dead to her, not merely transformed. Her mother, perhaps the whole village, had forbidden her return. A concerned Scanner summoned Robert Lion-612 for her. In the time it took him to cross the massive ship, her tears were all but gone.

"It's not a really high priority, Thandiwe." Bobby handed her wide male slippers. "Three years and you'll be underneath a real blue sky."

"Maybe," Thandiwe allowed, letting Bobby deflect a little. Now that she was an emotional male, she found some relief in avoiding terrible news. "If the other ship doesn't beat us to Veldt, first. If the planet is what our ancestors thought it would be. If. If. If." She sighed and glanced at him with frank appraisal. Her family's rejection had lifted the veil from her eyes. She saw now how her fisherboy attracted her. A mane so short as to be almost feminine. His slim build, wiry as a good huntress should be. Yet, he was big hearted and he valued life more than anyone she knew. *Well, wisdom doesn't come overnight.*

"Beloved," Bobby said into the gathering silence, "what do the thorns mean? You didn't even try to see your mother."

She glared at him from behind the mane that had fallen forward. "There was no point in trying to see my mother. I am dead to her."

"I explained that to her."

Thandiwe barked a short laugh. "There is no 'explaining' to my mother. You showed her a body in a jar. A body that you refused to allow her to bury properly."

"Because you weren't dead! You aren't dead."

Their eyes met. "You don't know what death means to my people. Death is but a moment in existence. And then there's a whole other kind of living. We are meant to go forward, to join our ancestors, to protect the living. But sometimes the dead are… confused. Especially if they are not buried properly or had lived evil lives."

"I know that—"

Thandiwe stood up and poked her fisherboy in the chest. "You know that, but you do not *believe* that. How many gazelles died with the huntresses that day? Seven or seventy? Do the clones all share the one soul or do they each have one made afresh when your replicators spit them out onto the range? My tribe accepts that… because it's just meat. You took me, remade me, rebuilt me, or even merely healed me… it doesn't matter. You claimed me and in that moment I was dead… I was no longer a natural being of my world."

Robert grabbed her thick fingers and, with two gentle hands, spread her fingers and pressed her palm to his uniform-covered chest. His wet eyes met hers. "I swear on my honor, Thandi, that your heart never stopped beating. Never. Not in here when the air turned to boiling soup. Not in the lifepod. Not while you healed in the vat. You fought for life every step of the way as the warrior that you are. Your heart never stopped beating, but my heart broke every time

I saw you lifeless in the Vat. I didn't claim you. You claimed me, Beloved; I love you."

Thandiwe felt oddly satisfied to hear him say that, yet she let the silence linger a few minutes longer as she thought of the books he had given her. "The thorns... they are our garlic. They are our salt... Obstacles for the dead. I was worried they might have trouble accepting that I was a male... but the truth is that doesn't matter to them. I am dead to them."

"You're not a vampire. Please don't make me regret giving you those stories," Bobby said softly. He stroked the wild bush of her mane. "Although, turning into a bat would be a really cool ability to have."

For some reason, this made her cry anew. This time, she allowed Bobby to wrap his arms around her. She accepted that she was weak, now, and marveled at her love's strength.

I should stop blaming him for saving me.

"I am sorry that I have been so... bitter."

"It's all right, Beloved." Bobby let her go and brushed her unruly mane from her eyes with his clean and neat Crew fingers. Feminine fingers, almost.

Thandiwe could even feel her balls sliding away from him. She had no idea what that meant, but it made her feel guilty. "I don't want to lose you, Bobby."

"I was afraid that I already had lost you." Bobby touched the bigger Cat's crotch and stroked the bulge there carefully. "I was afraid that this... would come between us."

"Does it?" She glared at him, challenging the crewman to admit that everything his shaman had told her was a lie.

"No. Dr. Jane explained what I am, right?" Bobby paused for the briefest of nods from Thandiwe. "So, I am okay with this. I know how to handle another male, don't you worry about that."

Thandiwe blushed at his gentle brag and she smiled briefly in spite of herself. "I want to be with you... but I cannot live my whole life on the Bradbury. I need real blue skies. But how can I set foot on

Veldt when my whole tribe rejects me?"

"Think about it, because of your condition, we could not have children before. You were the greatest, sexiest huntress… but you were sterile. Now, you are not sterile. You can still be a hunter, a warrior… it's… it's just another spear for you to learn how to use. I will make it work… *We* will work it out. Somehow."

Thandiwe closed her eyes and walked closer to the exposed metal plates of the partially repaired deck. It was an ugly gash in the illusion the Hunting Deck had fostered and the only reason the artificial intelligence let her in was that it saw her as Crew. Her world broken in so many places, but this tear looked exactly how she felt. Exposed. Weak. Ugly and unnatural. She stared at the scar until she was certain Bobby was close to her again. "I'm a male. I know that doesn't seem so bad to you… you've been a male all your life… and Crew… you *laugh* at our quaint gender roles and rules, I know. I was born to be a Colonist and those roles mean something. Dr. Jane says they are hard wired into my brain… one of the few things the Vat didn't have to grow back."

Bobby's gave a gentle laugh. "That's right, except for painkillers, your brain was untouched. Your brain might be awash in male hormones right now, but you are still you. You are exactly the same person that came in here months ago. Maybe a little traumatized, but the same."

She glared at him. He was in his brown uniform, but for the first time she realized that it was no longer spotless or wrinkle-free. Her heart melted a little when she realized that the look she'd first seen in his eyes today was mostly exhaustion. "What do you mean?"

"You still love me… just as I love you… male or woman… I love you. I want you."

Thandiwe looked at Bobby. "The whole time I was in the Vat," she spoke slowly and tried not to sound whiny, "I dreamed of you. I dreamed you were inside of me, smooth and clean. Hot against my belly and that the moment you came inside me, I'd know. I imagined shuddering with you as you poured yourself inside me."

"I've been inside you, Thandiwe."

"But always with a condom," she complained. "I never liked those."

"I can be inside you again."

Thandiwe's face twisted in an awkward expression of confusion and disgust.

"Don't be like that." Bobby's voice matched her own perceived whining. "I can show you some wonderful things. Will you please let me?"

"There's no future in it."

"There's more than one Lion Deck on the Bradbury. There's a Homeland Deck for Lions, you know that. There's mixed Cat Decks and Urban Decks for mixed species. We don't know what we'll find on Veldt."

She'd known that, of course. Thandiwe and all the children of the villages had seen all the species of the Bradbury in the Zoo during their formative years. Separate lives and separate cultures locked behind airlocks.

"Is it true, then?" She demanded. "Are the rumors of crew meddling true, then?"

"What do you mean by meddling?"

"That when we die, you remake us on another world. That when we die as a Lion, you make us reborn as an Avian or a Reptile. That you keep making us over and over again in some sort of great transmigration?"

Bobby blinked a few times as he seemed to process that. Thandiwe felt immediately stupid for even suggesting it, for he sort of laughed. "The graveyard does recycle the body... but not in the way you think... water and trace chemicals are reclaimed. Our magic boxes–"

"Scanners," Thandiwe injected.

"Right, our scanners. They take detailed medical information, which we file and examine. Otherwise, dead is dead for the Colonists."

Thandiwe's eyes narrowed. "What do you mean, *for the Colonists?*"

Before Bobby could say another word, an alarm went off, echoing across the vast empty deck. Bobby nearly jumped a meter into the air, even as Thandiwe's organized mind brushed aside the fight she was about to have with her Crewman. Even the most "primitive" Colonist understood what the twelve different alarms meant. This was one she'd thought she'd never hear.

The ship was under attack.

Bobby grabbed her thick hand in his, pulling her to the same lifepod they'd weathered the accident in. It was disguised, although she'd always known where it was, an open secret everyone ignored. Despite being frightened that she might see another breach, Thandiwe was overly aware of the unwelcome genitals bouncing around between her legs as she ran. She cursed herself for not wearing the tight underwear Bobby had suggested.

"The other ship… we tried hailing them," Bobby explained as they ran. "They seemed dead in the water."

The door opened with a squeal and they ducked inside. The instrument panel closest to the door was seared and melted, making Thandiwe realize again the hellfire that Bobby had carried her through. Bobby closed the door to the stale smelling compartment. Dim lights came on and a circuit began to sputter and spark. The lifepod designed for eight people, ten people if two people laid flat on the floor. In the training videos, the interiors were always spotless. Instead, soot and dried blood splatter decorated the floor and walls.

Thandiwe watched more panels spark as she felt her new maleness try to hide up inside her. Bobby had told her about the failing launch button, but she'd never seen the interior of the failed lifepod for herself. She looked at him with wide eyes. He nodded, forcing her to a seat before she could fall over.

"Don't touch it." He warned, needlessly. "Don't touch anything."

The restraining harness for the seat fell apart in her hands. "How long would these lifebelts protect us if…?"

Bobby just shook his head.

The pod's clamps began to rhythmically open and close. Thandiwe grabbed Bobby, their second embrace since she'd left the Vat as a male. Their first embrace with her new arms and hands and no tears in her eyes. Her genitals decided not to hide within her as his musk was pulled into her lungs. He was tired and unwashed, stressed. His scent was stronger than he normally let it go. He smelled like hope.

"Lifepods aren't a priority?"

Bobby shook his head again. "The journey is on its last leg, but the ship is on its last legs, too." He whispered, although there was no one to hear him but her. "We had to concentrate on rebuilding the shields and navigating with a thousand micro-course corrections." Bobby now embraced her back. "I wasn't allowed to tell you. We lost a few engineers, too."

"We were so close," she swore bitterly.

"We are still very close," he said firmly.

The ship shuddered beneath them and Thandiwe felt the first waver of artificial gravity pass through her, and she launched herself upright again. Bobby tried to make her sit again, but she grabbed a strap. "I am not dying sitting down."

The clamps complained for a moment and seemed to grind something before returning to their steady beat. The pulsing came up through the floor. A new sensation, a hardness between her anus and her scrotum, gripped her. Thandiwe wasn't sure what that meant, but she grabbed Bobby as he tried to pass by her. The Lioness instinctively pressed her groin into his.

The pressures of new, untested nerves sent signals to her brain. Cloth. Heat. He was soft, unprepared. Her penis was awakening. The touch was loud, the friction bright, and she wasn't even very hard yet. The tube of flesh projecting from her body began to fill with a maddening laziness. Her lungs began to pump air into her body, as if that would speed up the process.

Bobby was oblivious as he checked displays, pulling her with him a foot deeper into the pod as he called out to it. Pod could not speak. He found a datapad and confirmed his worries. The Crewman told Thandiwe that shields were down to 50% on this side of the ship. That the enemy seemed to only have three corsairs attacking them. "These seem slightly advanced, but unless there were other, hidden ships pushing an asteroid at us, we should be fine." He tried to draw away, but the Lioness held him firm.

Thandiwe could ignore the clamps' thumping, but Bobby's tense, frightened voice, even as he tried to make sense of things, could not be ignored, nor could the demands of the new phallic thing growing from her loins. She kissed Bobby's muzzle so hard, she could taste his blood before he could jerk his head back.

She pulled at his clothes, but the outfit and Bobby resisted. "You cannot help them," she whispered fiercely. "I do not want to die without tasting you as I am." She worked at his fly. Bobby surrendered to the moment with a grateful grunt and pulled at his zipper. The datapad clattered to the floor.

Their groins ground together and then their searching members found the excited flesh of each other. They pushed together lengthwise, holding each other. Their hands explored one another. Bobby pushed Thandiwe's chest up with one hand while pulling down on her ass with the other.

Thandiwe allowed herself to go passive when Bobby turned his full attention to her. This need felt so strange, as if the penis was both of her body and not of her body. Dr. Jane had hinted that her body would know how to do this. The fisherboy took control. Bobby bit the end off a little tube he pulled from a pocket and turned the tube around in his mouth, letting a few drops of gel bubble onto his fingertips.

His thumb massaged the fingertips of his furless and padless palm as his left hand squeezed her butt cheek encouragingly. Then those slick fingers wrapped themselves along the parallel shafts. Thandiwe gasped, grabbing the safety strap with both of her hands, as the more practiced male worked their flesh together in a firm but gentle grip. Dr. Jane's hygiene lessons had not included this bit of fun.

Thandiwe swayed from the safety strap with a death grip,

watching Bobby's round crew eyes watching her as the sensations made her face dance. Then the fingers tightened and he pumped down with more force. He matched the rhythm of the failing clamps and Thandiwe cried out in surprisingly deep roars of pleasure. She fought to keep her body from bucking; that would disrupt his rhythm. It took all that her divided attention could muster to let him work her flesh.

The male, the woman of her village had told her, almost always set the pace. So, too, had Bobby performed to expectations.

Bobby's hand moved from her ass to his mouth, where the little tube supplied more gel. Bobby returned to her butt and a slick, hot finger probed beneath her tail. He touched the hairless button and slowly spread a light coat of lube around her sphincter. A rush of panic and a shudder of ill-ease spiked her throat, but her tail did not slam downward.

His finger penetrated her. Something seemed to pop inside of her. He was inside of her! She thought that would never happen again, yet she was conflicted. This part felt wrong, but at the same time, Thandiwe felt her penis pulse forward as she released the strap holding them upright.

They fell into the seats and the huntress' claws extended, ripping into Bobby's uniform. The fisherboy yowled in protest. Thandiwe flipped him over and rudely pulled the fabric and circuitry apart. He whimpered eagerly. She wasn't sure, she didn't care. Desire had never pulled the Lioness out of herself before. Thandiwe needed to control something! Bobby was something that she could control.

She pulled his tail up roughly, with no more resistance from him than a yowl of surprise. She plucked the tube from the seat where it had fallen and followed his panting instructions to spread it on his hole and her own fleshy red thing, pushing her tawny sheath down to the base. Years of bawdy tales suddenly made sense to her.

Thandiwe pushed herself into Bobby, startled by the overwhelming sensation that focused her mind into her shaft. The ring of his flesh around her, the roar that came out of her throat unbidden. It felt like nothing she could comprehend. Yet, it also felt right.

The first inch was hard, but Bobby knew how to open himself up. The resistance collapsed and she was able to pump into him. The pounding clamps became competition of sorts. She fucked Bobby to their awful rhythm.

Then the clamps simply released and fell silent as the lifepod fell away from the ship.

They slapped to the floor as boosters ignited. Thandiwe, half mad with lust, opened her mouth wide and gripped Bobby's neck in her huge teeth. Her boyfriend gasped and tried to hold as still as possible as the tiny spikes near the base of her shaft slid into his asshole. The huntress chewed him from both ends, aware of the taste and scent of his blood. His whimpering excited her more than anything previously.

She could tell that he liked it in ways that she hadn't when he'd been in her tail hole.

Everything was new and different. When Bobby had been inside of her, Thandiwe's female body had welcomed him. It wasn't that she'd been passive; a Lioness was anything but that! But the warmth that spread out from her gonda had made her feel a part of everything.

But as a male, coming into Bobby, her passions felt outside of her own body. Her mind and her body did not become one. It was her and her penis, almost like the tube of flesh was a separate animal that she rode. She felt spent and empty, but strangely satisfied.

Thandiwe did not fully understand the impulse that slowly caused her to squeeze Bobby's throat like that. The women of her village had coyly suggested little nips in their storied conquests. Still, she was rewarded for her efforts when Bobby's smooth pink staff stood hard and tall from his loins. Crazy as it sounded, he seemed to like this utter domination.

The G-force pushed them down together, the artificial gravity unable to fully compensate. An invisible hand yanked at her scrotum. Their bodies were squeezed roughly and she exploded into Bobby a second time. He shuddered with his own release a second or two later as the rockets cut off along with the artificial gravity. Bobby's squirming body knocked them away from the floor.

They floated together, spent. Thandiwe began licking the scratches and prick-points of blood from Bobby's neck and shoulders. The coppery taste warmed and thrilled her softly. Thandiwe was drowsy, exhausted, and happy. She was ready to die, now. Her breath came in huge bellows, the taste of him in her mouth. The scent of him in her newly broad nostrils. It took a few seconds for her to think about him, to separate him from herself.

He was softly laughing and crying as they bounced gently in zero G. He pushed away from her, patting her hand away gently when she tried to pull him back. "Please, let's not do that when we've got a limited oxygen supply." He gasped and composed himself as he anchored himself to the pilot seat. "I think we've established that you're the Top."

"I'm sorry," she said, not feeling very contrite. She supposed she might, later. If they survived this little adventure. The afterglow her ladyparts had given her had been warming, spreading throughout her body. Now, as a male, that energy seemed inverted, as if she were cooling now. The energy seemed to flow out of her body, causing her to dissolve in the air. Although, that might have been the zero gravity. "I just didn't want to die without…" Her mind felt dull and she couldn't think of a better turn of phrase. "I just needed to fuck you and fuck you hard before I died."

Bobby sniffled as he belted himself in the pilot seat. "Well, I can't say I wasn't above hoping we'd get past that awkward second first time. I just never thought I'd need an accident report filled out afterwards."

Thandiwe kept her mouth shut. Her mother had never told her what to say after sodomizing one's boyfriend in a deathtrap. Did he want an apology for fucking him so hard or for not fucking him sooner?

Bobby looked back after making a few commands on the keyboard and smiled. His wet, tearing eyes shining like not-too-distant stars. There was no anger in his eyes. Her lover waved her forward. Thandiwe used a few hand holds and came up behind him, hoping that these were the tears of joy she'd heard much about.

"I've moved us within the shadow of the loose FTL engine," Bobby said, asserting control like a good Crewman would. Thandiwe was not only too tired to argue, but she had to admit that this was a job Crew was best prepared for. She looked out into space through windows Bobby had revealed with a flip of a switch or two. Her left hand brushed her shrinking member, unconsciously. She and her betraying flesh felt unreal against a black void.

Arcs of bright light leapt between fighter ships, illuminating them and part of the great hull of the Bradbury. The arcology designed sections created weird shadows in the flashes. The Bradbury did not look like the bush she'd always imagined, but more of a rope with many knots. "The other ships concentrated fire on the Crew section," Bobby supplied helpfully. "I think they need restocking of Colonists. Or maybe they are trying to discourage us from making a 'supply run' on their ship."

Thandiwe looked at Bobby in surprise. "Surely, we wouldn't resort to pirating from another ship."

Bobby smiled and gave her direct eye-contact. Taking control seemed to have rejuvenated him, despite the blood still dripping from his neck. Suddenly, he was more than a cute and exotic example of manhood. In his world, she appreciated anew, he had more than his share of strengths. "No. But we would salvage a dead or dying ship. The Bradbury is on its last legs and that near miss did not help. Even hulled and open to vacuum, that other ship might have genetic tampers and water that we could use to better our odds." He fussed with a control that seemed to respond sluggishly. "And, we are obligated to rescue any survivors we find, even if that puts a strain on our system."

The Huntress kissed his head, just below the hairline of his short mane. Thandiwe tasted blood and sweat, little globules of which danced in the air around him. Her basic lifepod training began to assert itself. "Let me get the first aid kit." She rummaged in the back of the pod, enjoying the weightlessness, a little yet grateful at the same time that she hadn't eaten much. There were two kits, one empty with scorch marks and the other full and untouched.

They hadn't even restocked the medical stores. This gave her pause, but she pushed past the issue. It was just another reminder that neither Crew nor councils were gods.

"Thanks," he answered, his eyes shuttling between his readings and the porthole. "Looks like there's only one raider left. By the Xristos, he's fast. Shots are going wild. Our guys have chased him away from the Bradbury. Complete opposite direction from his own ship."

Thandiwe nodded, seeing the wisdom. The pilots would not want to be lured into a trap, especially if the newcomer was better armed than the Bradbury. Also, to get back to its own arcology ship, the raider could not be allowed to come close to the Bradbury.

She began wiping Bobby's wounds clean as he stayed focused on the two sources of information. This small act of caregiving made her feel manly without resentment.

This introspection made her look forward, quite literally and figuratively. The black canvas of space was an inviting place for deep thinking.

And fear.

Three pinpricks of sparks danced across the shadows and darkness. She'd have dropped the cleaning gauze if there'd been gravity to take it from her hand. "Ships, up ahead."

Bobby glanced to the shadow of the huge FTL engine that had nearly killed them a few weeks ago. "No, that's just the FTL engine bay that broke off. We've put robo-tugs on it. You probably saw them making a course correction."

"I thought we didn't need that." Thandiwe found herself as angry at the inanimate engine for her injuries and transformation as she was with the new ship.

"We don't," Bobby said, turning back to watch the real action.

"But on the off chance Veldt needs to be terra-formed, FTL engines can be converted to that end."

"I want to be a fighter pilot," Thandiwe said. Her own world had not seemed very welcoming of late.

Bobby smiled wickedly and she saw that in his reflection. "You got my vote. I've always liked a man in uniform."

Both pleased and uneasy with his answer, she formulated a reply. Before she could answer, more glittering sparks appeared. "Bobby, seriously, I see ships."

Bobby gave a serious look. "You do have better eyes than me. But it could just be sparks from asteroids hitting together." He started hitting his datapad in cryptic ways with a bald finger. "Sensors are blocked by the FTL engine. Let's see… there, FTL computer and systems online. Camera system coming online… forward view, extreme magnification. Augmenting with false coloring."

"Shit," they said in unison at the datapad.

They could see many dozen small fighter craft, weaving their way around the larger pieces of space debris. This was twice the compliment that the Bradbury could muster.

"They're sneaking in through the sensor shadow from the FTL drive," Bobby cursed. "The remaining ship is just distracting the Bradbury from the incoming."

"Can't we warn them?" Thandiwe growled, surprised that Crew "magic" had its limits.

Bobby shook his head no. "We cannibalized communications for sensors years ago. They rigged up old style radio broadcast so the ship, the probes and the fighters could communicate with each other. The lifepods were never upgraded and these controls can only talk to machines. The only people we can probably talk to are the enemy."

Thandiwe hissed and then roared in frustration. Bobby didn't even blink at this. His training kept him focused.

"The enemy and that damn nacelle," Bobby said tightly. "I'm in the FTL controls, but I can't access any radio transmissions here. If they salvaged that from the nacelle, it must be a stand alone."

Bobby was not the huntress that she was. Becoming a male would not change that. Her mind took in the FTL device, a long thick spear pointing towards the enemy and her oncoming minions. "Bobby, you can control the FTL engine?"

"Yes," he said absently, playing with figures and numbers across his pad. "But it has no weapons."

"It's pointed right at the enemy fleet and their mother ship."

"But it has no weapons," Bobby snapped back, annoyed at having to repeat himself with so much at stake.

"How long to restart the FTL engines?"

"Seconds," Bobby said. "It's easier to leave them on standby and the fuel is collected as we cross slip fractures and... Thandiwe, I know you want to help, but I'm trying to find a way to contact the Bradbury so we can warn them!"

Thandiwe kept her cool. Bobby was male, but he was Crew. He had never learned how to properly listen to a real warrior. "Look, that FTL engine got us into this mess." She said gently but firmly, "I think it should get us out of this."

Bobby turned to snap at her, but then the logic of what she said began to sink in.

"Thrust your spear into its center mass," Thandiwe repeated her mother's favorite hunting lesson in Southern Heartland and then in Crew, "Thrust your spear into its heart!"

"The robo-tugs could never..." Then he stopped and smiled viciously. "I love you, Thandiwe!" he cried out as he turned back to the control panel and pulled another datapad. He drew up the blue screen with six blocks of white numbers. "I need you to take this and use the tugs to bring the nacelle to this orientation."

Thandiwe blinked at him. "I don't know how to do that." Her lifepod training hadn't covered using datapads.

"Sorry, I forgot." Bobby made some quick calculation on the fly. "Here, when the numbers approach zero, hit the red button next to that number. Don't worry about the last two numbers. They are for tumble and relative distance to the Bradbury."

Thandiwe nodded and took the pad. In the back of her mind, she was pleased that Bobby had forgotten that she was something of a "savage." If they survived this, she was going to show him her gratitude. "I love you, too, my fisher boy."

"Then every scratch and bite mark was worth it," he said lightly. "There we go, engine check good. Batteries at 75%, Fuel almost at ignition temperature. Ready to go in twenty seconds. The engine doesn't even have to hit them... the gravimetric wake alone... How are those numbers?"

"Three numbers at near zero. Now four."

"Good," Bobby said. "Release and return those tugs, we might need them later."

Thandiwe nodded. Right after she'd hit the red button for each tug, three buttons had appeared for each. Release was an option. She selected that and two more options appeared. She selected Return and then the Engage button when that appeared. That task completed, Thandiwe took a deep breath and suddenly felt as if she had inhaled a wet sock. "Are we good with air?" she asked casually. She was, after all, ready to die for her people.

"No, we're good," Bobby assured her. "That's just stress smell in a small pod. Maybe a trace of the gasses from the accident."

Thandiwe wasn't sure she believed him, but she admired his stoicism. "We're ready to fire?"

"Yes," Bobby said, "I'm just writing a quick log entry about what we did and why." He took her pad and pulled up another screen. The approaching ships were on it in the false colors that made them stand out against the void. "The book says I should try to communicate with them first..."

"I have read no such book," Thandiwe said simply, glad to play the savage.

Bobby turned his head to share a quick, grim smile. "Your spear is lined up, the FTL is powered up. Hit the launch button."

Thandiwe looked at the pad. There was no telling who piloted those ships. There was no telling which species was coming out to meet them armed. No telling what societies they represented. She knew them only as desperate, reckless people who had their sights on her home.

"No," Thandiwe told him, "this is your kill. Finish them."

Bobby nodded with a tight smile, showing that he understood her display of respect. "Launch," he said, without further ado.

Thandiwe meant to ask if they were too close, but instantly, a hole full of rainbows and madness opened up in front of them and then it was too late for questions.

***

Dr. Jane came to them, weeks later, very early in the morning. They had chosen the reclaimed Heartland deck from the other Ark Ship, which they learned had been called The Correct. Although more advanced, it was of the same general module design as the Bradbury and many of the surviving decks dedicated to the different environments and habitats were wholly salvageable. Beneath a different blue sky with the shadows of many small moons no one on the Bradbury had ever truly walked under, Dr. Jane felt a thrill of seeing something new. This was the sky of Nightmare, the world the mutineers on the Correct had abandoned. A nearly perfect world, they'd explained. Except for the earthquakes that ran as regularly as Earth's lunar tides. Something no amount of terraforming could solve.

She walked into Thandiwe's hut on the Lion Village deck which had been built for Felines that had been stranded on the world named Nightmare, forgetting that the hut would not announce her approach the way a good room would.

She ducked out almost immediately. The Tiger's tail and ears spoke of sudden embarrassment.

Thandiwe's gruff voice called out, "What is it?"

Bobby tittered a bit as Dr. Jane composed herself. From the doorway, the Tigress said, "The captain said to tell you that the Correct's supplies of genetic tampers are now available for us. In light of your actions, he is allowing you use the tampers to restore your sex—"

"No! I'm good!" she panted from inside the darkened hut.

Dr. Jane hesitated. "Are you sure?"

Thandiwe said nothing, letting the sound of slapping flesh and Bobby's heaving gasps for breaths speak for her. Her mouth was full of her man's neck. Suddenly, Bobby made a choking sound that the Huntress had learned was a precursor to his orgasm. She'd learned how to delay her own release under Bobby's expert instructions. Thandiwe roared, hearty and satisfied, and they both spilled their seeds. The Huntress, inside of her man, and Bobby between their slick bodies. Bobby whimpered and tried to catch his breath.

"Are you sure?" Dr. Jane asked again from outside their hut.

"No, I'm good," Thandiwe replied in as normal voice as possible. "Thank the Captain and the council for thinking of me… but could you ask if we could try Bobby as a female for a while? It was his killing shot, after all."

"Wha—?"

"Nothing, Bobby," Thandiwe said in a teasing whisper. "Go back to sleep."

Dr. Jane did not move from the doorway, but glanced in with a smile. After a few moments, Bobby was snoring and Thandiwe was almost ready to join him.

"There were six Lionesses frozen in the Correct," The Tigress observed, looking up at the alien sky. "As mutineers, the Captain has a great deal of discretion in how they are handled. And this village does seem rather empty. If you are truly comfortable as a male, the council suggested that you might wish to have them as concubines."

Thandiwe rolled Bobby off her onto the mat and approached the doorway on her still tender footpads. Dr. Jane took in her wild mane with a knowing glance and the Huntress found herself blushing. Together, they stared at the fake sky as if they'd never seen it's like before. A second sun had begun to rise in the east. Nightmare's sky.

"Wives?" The Lioness asked after the sky became an even brighter blue. "You expect me to take wives?"

Dr. Jane smiled. "I am hoping to get you and Robert to take these women as wives. Three each. And when your children and his children have offspring; those grandchildren will both be yours and Bobby's."

The Lion grunted thoughtfully. "A tribe of our own… I must admit, that appeals to my ego, but I am not sure what Bobby would say. This might upset him."

Dr. Jane tried not to smile, but Thandiwe knew her friend would fail. "Well, I've explained to you Heterosexuality, Homosexuality, and Bisexuality, to you, right?"

Thandiwe glanced back at her first binary sunrise, wondering where this was going. "Right…"

Dr. Jane smiled, wide and delighted. "Well, in the name of genetic diversity, let me tell you about Polysexuality."

Wild Dog

Franklin Leo

I tilt back my beer and let frothy suds stain the hair of my whiskers, chirps escaping my throat. Around me, animals and humans talk, shake hands, and eye each other in curiosity. Some even sniff, checking the other for familiar scents. The pianist on stage moves into his fifth number, as several folks get up to dance. It's a good piece, so I hum my calls in time with the tempo, just as the bartender slides me another beer.

"How much more noise you going to make, Riley?" he asks. His long panther tail sweeps dust off the shelves behind him.

"How long until this place gets sold?"

"Not for another few weeks." He's polishing a glass. I sniff the air, hooting a couple of calls as the front door opens. "How'd that date with the vixen go?"

I snort, but it comes out a sharp squeak. "What date?"

"Really, now. Her?"

"Wanted to keep herself clean, she said. No new changes, I guess."

"If you're into that, I suppose. Damn shame."

Maybe. Someone knocks me in the tail, but I ignore it and stay focused on the rising music. It'd kill to own this place, I think. The vixen falls from my mind, and lifting up my glass, I let empty suds kiss my lips and cause me to wince. Dry.

A paw touches me on the back, with dull claws tracing the line of my shoulder. "Helps if there's anything in there. You finished with that, or can I buy you another?"

Her voice pulls me from the glass, and when I look, I find that it's Samantha. She's smiling past her spotted Dalmatian muzzle with enough sarcasm to bring down the building. My tail wags like a puppy's, while hers remains still, tall. She's hunted me down through the crowd, prey to her domestic instincts.

"Sure, if I'm covering yours," I say.

The dog shrugs her shoulders, and she waves back at the bartender for another round. He notices and gets to work whilst she sits. "Don't see you around here anymore. When I do, you seem to be enjoying yourself." A nod towards my row of glasses gets me to flick my ears. "Someone let you down, or is this normal?"

"I hear it's normal for wild dogs to drink sporadically, but they never said how it'd affect my alcoholism." I wait for my new drink to come, and then I down it to the middle.

"Part of the change, huh? Better than growling at strangers, I suppose." She winks, before nuzzling my ear.

And my mind explodes. I chatter over the thrumming noise of conversation and blush beneath my distinctly mottled fur. My mind says, *keep going. Ask her about her day.* My body, on the other hand, would like to take her home and see what her muzzle's capable of doing. She traces her claws along my side, as though feeling the muscle for any flaws. My tail wags, ears perk, and—

"When I changed, they told me I'd never drink again. My dad, however, had a dog who could outdrink anyone under the table, so here I am."

The ache in my groin ceases just as I remember I'm out in public. Maybe I am drunk. Buzzed. "Geeze, wasn't that bad for the guy? Was he a horse?"

"Girl, actually, and a lab. She lived to be about sixteen," she says.

The jazz on stage ends as the leopard playing stops for the next rotation. The bar quiets down, but clinking glasses ring the air and keep the vibe going.

We talk through the changing musicians as if we were alone. Not in some club hidden beneath the street, but in our own place, where musicians could play out their souls and watch us bob in rhythm.

Finally, she nuzzles me once more, startling me once again. The touch everyone longs for. "As fun as watching you drown yourself may be, want to get out of here? I mean, go find some food or something?"

I turn my head to see her gazing at me through hazel eyes. Her floppy ears stand perked, forward, as if she were begging. My own ears have been radio'd onto her for the last half hour. For a moment, we're two alphas. Two members of the same family. "Sure. Know a place?"

She takes her glass, a tall martini piece filled with something green, and ingests it all in one quick lap. "Do I know a place, as if I'm some sort of child, Riley."

And that was how it started, two dogs with nowhere to go without the other.

***

Outside, the clouds open to reveal dazzling stars. Diana releases me from her jaws as my fur, soft, grows and shines with magic in dark hues of black and brown. My claws pop out from human nails against the car's creaking hood, and sharp teeth curve from beneath my lips. A howl builds in me until I can't hold it in. All that escapes are hoots, chirps, and squeaks.

I bite her in return, and she screams. Not in agony, no. We make sweet, sweet love, and a tail wags out from behind me, tells me who I am. That I'm wild. That I'm just another animal trying to find the olive to his just poured martini. They say that African Wild Dogs are rare these days. Low in numbers, but good with staying together. I dig it, and the instincts flood in as I accept their call. The connection and bonding, the staying imprinted upon each other. It calls me, and so does she: we make a pack, even with only our own two hides. We'll be together forever, connected through life.

It only hurts so much more than when she leaves me to become a lion.

***

I bite into the steaming hot pastrami sandwich, while Samantha helps herself to a Philly, cheese staining part of her lips. It's five in the morning, and the line of hungry drinkers still trying to sober up keeps growing and growing. Above us, neon casts down an unhealthy glow on both of our pelts and the unkempt wrappings of grease-stained wax paper.

"I get why there are so many dogs, but you'd think that someone would become…I don't know. What about a sea lion in Nevada, or a tiger in New York?"

"Have you seen any tigers?" I ask. "I mean, actual tigers."

"Only a few. My neighbors were tigers when I was younger."

"Well, there you go." Another bite sends pickle juice spitting into my throat.

"What about you? Does anyone mark you down in their bucket-list of sightings?"

"What do you mean?" I can't help a hoot escaping. Sometimes, they just come out.

"You know what I mean," she says. "Wild Dogs. Not from around here, noisy, going extinct. You have a charity for yourself, or…?"

A fox at the counter turns, as though she were listening in. She looks at my ears, my mottled fur. She spins back around to hide her curiosity.

"I guess. Animals definitely notice it."

"And does that bother you?"

"Why should it?"

She smiles again, causing her spots to shift along her cheeks, before placing a paw on my wrist. "Because it can."

We finish our breakfast, me sucking down a straw full of Coke, when the sun starts poking its head up from over some cars. The human kid, walking around picking up our trash, nods with his small burger hat when he takes away our tray.

"My mom thought I needed to get help when I changed," Samantha says. "Everyone ended up a housecat except me. I loved it. They'd turn a corner, and I'd let loose a bark that got them screeching."

I laugh and nearly spit out the Coke I just drank. "Why are you talking to me?" I ask.

"Why am I talking to you? You come without a filter, too?"

"You walked up tonight as if I stepped on your turf. Why'd you choose me out of everyone back at JJ's?"

"Well I hate to be the bearer of bad news," she says, "but I'd like to take you to my place. Would that be okay, or do I have to be interrogated about that, too? We've known each other for what? Four years, now?"

But she's never spoken to me. I bite my lip and feel as though I've thrown myself to the wolves, as though I'm only here to make her stand out. She eyes me with squinted brows and cupped paws. Her tail isn't wagging anymore. "What do you think?" I say.

"Me?" She straightens up. Leaning close, I smell the food on her breath, and let out a squeak that pulls my tail into a wag. "I think I'd fuck you here just to see who howls."

She doesn't need to say anymore. At once, all of the sounds I've been holding in escape, like calling to a pack I never was a part of. We take our drinks and head to the car. She's driving a sporty jeep that has room for tails beneath the seats, and the windows stay open. Her hood's covered in mud.

"Let's take our time," I say, and she takes my paw without words as if it were always meant to be.

***

We're kissing on the couch, my claws tracing over her warm, soft flesh. Her hair trails down and back in a mix of mullet and mane, despite it being so human and unattractive to me. Things start picking up, though. Chirping like a bird, I let her feel over my sheath and squeeze my packed and tucked balls. She bites at my neck and starts to grind, drunker than anyone I'd ever been with. She bites me, soft at first, before I yelp and howl. We build into a hump that's stronger, faster than Diana could have ever given me. I squeeze her hips. She licks my neck. A bite, and when I bite back, she screams. Our fun ends like a burst balloon falling to the floor on some big birthday.

In the morning, she tells me that it's okay, that she's fine. She's woken up a Wild Dog, a queen to my king. I'd give her everything I have and more, start a pack with her so we can have children to fill a grand house with.

But all she hears is Wild, and the dream gets shot down, and when she runs, I can only squeak and cry, call out her name. Instead, the name that comes out is Diana.

***

We see each other a week later when I walk out of the restroom and find her looking over an old ID. Human, my image brings a smile to her lips. Brown eyes, short hair. The face that so obviously doesn't match the animal I've become. I move closer, and her ears perk towards me. I don't even have to say her name.

"Henry Davis. You were cute. Cuter now, I think."

I make my way across the small club, ignoring the stacking of chairs and stools. Closing. "Thanks. I always needed someone to boost my ego."

She waves the ID again before sliding it into my wallet. "Why the name change?"

"Needed something new. Can't hold on to what's not real. Ready to leave this place?"

We pay our bill and head on down to the same diner that Sam took me to before. We order the same, then head to her place. I get the door for her as she waits wagging with her bag of fries in her muzzle, like a good dog. I don't hide what it does to me, and I nuzzle her neck before letting her inside. Tonight, I've found myself chittering less and less.

We make it to the living room before the food gets thrown aside and we clear the floor for sex. Sam makes the first move. I sit on the couch and watch her, shirt undone, as she turns on the music and her gas-fueled fireplace. Her apartment is modeled after a late 19th century fire house, and in one corner stands a golden bronze pole like that of a fire unit's garage. Instead of sliding down it, she uses it to help her get undressed, before riding it like a dancer who knows she's being watched.

I take my beer, open it, and let half of its suds fill my stomach. By now, the room only flickers. My ears feel it the worst, and fidget like bored children as a chirp finally leaves my throat.

"My father was the funny one who did this," she says about the room. "Think it's cheesy?"

"It must certainly make you feel at home," I say.

The Dalmatian bites back her grin. "Shut up."

Naked, she steps forward and strides towards me, a ballerina presenting herself. Her years of dancing reveal curves and muscle that I've never seen, and before I know it, we're on the ground, both of us naked and twining our legs around the other's body. She covers me with wet kisses and noses between the muscles, while I hoot and squeak. Partly barreled, my chest sticks out, and she nibbles where she can while being slow and cautious. I use my tongue to get under her muzzle, and she grabs my cock before it can finish sliding out of its coverage.

The first thing she does is take it in her teeth, and I yelp. Not hard, of course, but it makes me want to bite her back, and it takes every inch of me not to do so. It's the first time I realize how close I've come to being infected, but I claw the sandalwood flooring to try and hold myself from coming.

She stops. "What's wrong?"

"Nothing." I pant, close to orgasm but also feeling the sting. "It's nothing. Just a startle."

"Did I do something?"

"No, you didn't. Maybe. Easy on the teeth, maybe?"

Samantha sits up. The sexy seductress performance drops, as her legs unfurl from under me like a blooming flower. "Should we stop? I didn't meant to bite too—"

"No, it's fine," I say. "You didn't break the skin. Besides, I don't feel like I'm changing. We don't have to stop. Do you want to?"

"No," she says. Her paw takes my neck and pulls me close to her lips. "I really don't."

Placing her on her back, I move my way on down and whimper soft music. I kiss her stomach and abs with gentle enough licks, that by the time I reach her vagina, she's wet and shivering. Whines escape her throat, matching my own like true Wild Dog fashion. Maybe she's the one changing, I think.

"You ready?" I ask.

"Am I ready? Must you ask me about everything, dog?"

I plunge my muzzle into her, and her whines burst out into a throated gasp, ending in chitters. My throat silences itself to make room for every piece of her, and I nose in deeply, tongue unfolding long. Diana's out of my mind. Instead, Samantha howls and waits for me, clearly the one I was meant for.

When she comes, I lap every bit of her fluids up. She pets me with those soft paws of hers as I whine and play the part. I ignore the soreness of my member, the sting of what I now understand was from that of a bite.

In the morning, she tells me I've acted the quietest that I have ever been.

***

When I wake up, she's gone into the shower without me. A plate of nachos sits waiting for me on the counter. The cheese has turned the chips soggy and wet.

The night swims through my mind like a bad memory mixed with feelings of rejoice. The sensation of having another canid with you rests like no other, and having her talk to me with such verboseness always gets me riled.

But I also realize what this could mean. Her chitters and chirps, the way her howl sung so unmusically. Could she be at last changing into a Wild Dog, something I've been waiting for and questioning? I've nicked her once with a claw. Should I be worried?

I get up and head for the nachos. After a few minutes, I'm well into a pawful when she exits the bathroom and lets steam simmer along the carpet. Towels cover her lithe body while her tail wags behind. I scan her figure to see if she's showing any signs of the signature fur, the tall, listening ears. Nothing's changed, and playing along, she shimmies out and hints at the nudity beneath.

"Good morning," she says. Her voice sings through the air as she touches me on the shoulder with a nose rub.

"Doing okay?" I mouth around the layers of meat and chips. "You seem a bit jazzed."

"Truth? I feel gorgeous. How about you? You slept like a rock last night."

"Peachy," I say. Again, I search to see what's different past my spotted muzzle. She's not chirping, that's for sure.

Samantha pulls up one of her stools and sits across from me. Her eyes look into mine, and she can't stop herself from smiling. Her spots decorate her cheeks like small twinkling buttons, as my own fur seems to tickle and itch. Maybe I should take a shower myself. "Sorry if I freaked you out last night. I really didn't mean to get you that hard."

"It's okay. You know what they say. A bite's like messing with a grenade."

"Well, when you have teeth like ours…" She steals a chip from the plate. "I have to go to work and pick up some things, but I was hoping you'd stick around. I did feed you, after all."

I smirk, and let myself ease into a sigh. "Really? You're not done with me yet?"

She rolls her eyes and places a paw on my wrist. "Do you want me to be done?"

I don't answer, and she stays silent, waiting. Neither of us seem to be howling or chirping, the sign for bonding. Eventually we finish the nachos, myself worried whether I've done something wrong, and she pulls over a gallon jug filled to the top with water. "I'll be back. Take your meds. Try not to miss me too much."

She dresses and tosses her towels in the basket. Her fur smells warm from the shampoo, and when she passes, I can't help but lean in for a sniff along her neck. I nuzzle her for a good second, before she leaves. Her scent continues to drive my tail into wagging until the sound of her car tells me she's out for good.

I look down my muzzle, oddly light to my eyes in color, when a text buzzes my phone. "*Surprise, surprise. You do like me.*"

I smile. "*Only a little. Try not to take too long.*"

"*Hardly. You look cute like this, by the way. It suits you.*"

The text sits with me for a moment, smile still hanging, until something punches me in the stomach and drops my throat to my chest. Like this? What *this* could she mean?

I drop the phone and rush for a mirror. Any mirror, I think, but in shock, I'm wandering around the apartment, stumbling on a footstool and glancing around. At last, I enter the bathroom and wipe away a thin layer of steam that still coats the glass from Samantha's shower. The reflection clears, and before me stands myself, eyes wide and muzzle hanging open.

And then I see it. My ears, once tall and perked in a permanent stand, now hang in a forward droop that mimics the flop of common Dalmatians. I try and make them stand, hoping they do, but they flop around like limp leaves, ends colored black. My fur, once a botched mix of tan and black, now resembles a cream of white, punctuated by various sizes of round, decorative blotches.

I realize why I never saw any changes in her. All this time, she's nibbled and nicked me alongside the bite on my cock that cut our love-making short last night. My calls and chirps have been reducing steadily, leaving me silent unlike before. Looking in the mirror, now, I see my eyes seem to brighten, the brown I once had returning as moisture glints on my nose. While Samantha walked away without a single change affecting her, I've ended up taking a piece of her with me, and it's making me a common dog the longer I stare myself down.

That shortly comes to an end, however, as I slump and let my body collapse. Every dog has to have his first fainting spell, I suppose. My tail even shakes off the last of Wild Dog fur in the process, creating a sad and shaven pile of fuzz.

***

I open my eyes to find myself still lying on the rug of her bathroom. Around me, the apartment is silent, and distant birds call while someone barks down the street. Using my nose, I check to see if Samantha's returned, if even for a moment. The only scent that remains is my own.

Which means I'm by myself, unless she comes walking in. I feel up to my ears and find them still soft and floppy. My mind fixes the image of black fur on them to complete the spotted muzzle before me. Everything smells much stronger, now, and I glance down. My clothes seem to have grown; my frame is much thinner, leaner, than before.

I get up. The open window of her bathroom shows that it's late afternoon, and the neighborhood is in full swing while neighbors water down sidewalks or play games out in the street. The funny thing about being an animal is that the world is your playground, if you choose to make it one, but I focus on getting dressed and out, first, as much as the dog-like idea of play seems to inspire pressing joy inside of me. I need to find Samantha and see what we can do about all of this. Grabbing some clothes, taking my meds, the thought of play sits in my mind as I wonder whether it's me, or if such a thought is just a joke.

The only place I know Sam frequents is JJ's, and soon, I'm off towards Old Towne in no time. I reach the corner around four, when the clock tower at Benson's chimes the hour and signals folks to head home. Humans and animals take their time moving in shuffling herds. Briefcases clap against each other, while phones ring and claws scratch the pavement.

JJ's, however, stands silent on the corner with its hot coffee sign switched off for the day. At night, it'll return to a welcoming glow. My car stays parked out front, and a citation sits waiting for me pressed beneath my windshield wiper.

I go inside to find different people staffing the same positions. A rat works the register while several dogs cook behind the counter. A Labrador is taking orders, and she seems happy to find that the store is quiet for once.

"Excuse me." I walk up to the rat, paws fumbling in my pockets for change. "Have you seen a Dalmatian come in here anytime recently?"

"Dalmatians come in here all the time." The rat speaks quickly, biting back what I imagine are squeaks. "Got any names?"

"Samantha. Don't know the last."

"Saw her last night," The Lab passes and glances at me, snapping her gum.

"She come by yet?"

"Come back later, maybe. She usually visits before going dancing."

Of course, but I don't have that time. An itch tickles me downstairs, as I catch the smell of Lab building in my register. I look the waitress over before I palm the rodent a bill, and turn back out the diner to get into my car.

I'm turning into a dog, and Samantha's nowhere to be found. Yes, I'd been a Wild Dog for years, but knowing that part of my life was over for something different and off just made me whine. Literally. I know that if I don't get bitten by a Wild Dog soon, the change to Dalmatian will stay until the next chance I get.

I'm pulling the ticket off my car's window, however, when I spot a white and black spotted canine making her way down the sidewalk.

She's carrying bags of clothes as though she's just been on a massive shopping spree, and her eyes are covered by reflective aviators made particularly for her muzzle shape. It's Samantha, and she doesn't have a care in the world, moving along the street like she owns the place. Like she's made away with owning a new dog and is looking forward to his new fur coat.

"Hey." I step around my car, keys back in my pocket. "What are you doing?"

Samantha turns, slow at first. Her nose catches wind, and when she's finally able to see me, her eyes light up behind the glasses. She comes over just to nose me, and I catch her tail wagging. She smiles. "Decided to get up this morning, did you?"

"Can we talk for a moment?" The whine slips out again without much help from my tongue.

"What are we doing right now? Flirting?"

"I mean privately." I point to my car.

She smiles again, endearingly if not considerate. "Hey, I get it. We did things. Doesn't mean I'm ready to get serious with you, though."

"It's not about that," I say. "It's about…my ears."

"Your ears?" she asks.

"Yes, my ears."

The dog winces, before rolling her eyes. "I see more than your ears, hon. What? Have a problem with the new you?"

"Yes, and no. Please, I'd like if we could talk for a moment. Cut me some slack, here."

"All right. All right. Let's go to my car. I parked in the lot by Claro's." Samantha slides her glasses from her muzzle, and like that, she's the dog I've known, tail wagging behind.

She leads me to where I can only expect her car is after I slap the ticket back on mine. Her hips sway, bobbing that lean tail behind her. I can't stop myself from looking down and panting. Realizing I'm doing just that, I bite my lip and turn. No one across the street or near us even seems to care. The couple of Dalmatians fit in with the moving crowd.

"You know, you're not the first to come back. Does that mean I was good?" she asks. Samantha can't help but rub up against me.

"Are you really trying to flirt with me right now?" I say.

"Maybe. Haven't decided yet."

We stop in front of her convertible, which I can now smell as hers thanks to her fur lining and decorating the upholstery. "So should I put the roof up, or are we going anywhere?"

"Roof, please."

She brings out her keys and hits the button. Like me, the vehicle shifts itself into a new form, before we enter, me sitting passenger as she takes the driver's seat.

"Okay, what's up?"

"I need you to help me change back," I say. "I want to get rid of this. All of it."

Like flipping a switch, the dog's eyes narrow. "Hold on. You don't like it?"

"I tried to tell you. Last night, when I hesitated."

"No, you didn't. You told me everything was fine, but now you're asking me to help you go and fuck something else."

I wince. Harsh, but it's the truth. Why try and hide it? "I've only known myself as a Wild Dog. It's me, who I am. Do you know how hard it'll be to get others to see me as me? What about work, or getting carded?"

"Your ID has you human, genius." A growl slides from her throat. "And I did this because I liked you."

"Then why don't you want to help me? Why act like you owe me nothing?"

"Because I don't," she says. Her bite reveals itself behind her rising lips. "You know what? Take this as karma. All of you guys think you can walk all over us. Think you can take what you want and leave us to hang. And when we actually like you, and want to be with you? You shut us down, or do something nuts like this, so, take your new dog-ass as a parting gift. I'm sure you'll find someone else to bang and bite you."

"What? You're going to leave me like this?" I say. My voice cracks into a snarl that turns shoulders across the street. I cover my muzzle. Too late.

"Do you have any idea what we'd have to do to change you? I can't just—"

A tap comes from behind me, and startles us both into a short spasm before turning. Samantha hits the ignition and lowers the windows.

"Is everything okay?" the officer asks. He leans down and in our view, muzzle a heavy jowl that drools saliva onto the unseen sidewalk. I wince from the odor reeking from his gums.

"We're fine, sir. Just having a spat," Samantha says.

"No, everything's not fine," I say. "She bit me and made me into a dog." I lean back, letting him see the baggy clothes drenched on my form. Yeah, goodbye lean muscle.

Rather than sympathize, the Great-Dane looks away, red flushing his ears. "Sir, what you and your partner do inside of the bedroom is your business and yours alone."

"But it's not. She infected me." A growl parts my lips to show teeth.

"Sir, I'm going to have to ask you to calm down."

"That's what I'm trying to tell him." The Dalmatian snorts a laugh.

"Take care, then," he says, and leaves me watching with my muzzle hanging wide open.

"You're welcome," Samantha says. "Now get out of my car."

Does she really think she can get away with this? My throat clenches as another growl rises from my chest. My paws tighten into two hard fists. How am I the victim of this? How am I the one being told to walk away?

"You stubborn, traumatized, spoiled—" I'm cut off mid-turn when a fist knocks straight into my face. My muzzle seems to snap, and I yelp. Knuckles cut beneath my fangs. Before I can think what's happened, I'm out on the sidewalk thanks to the flimsy latch of her door.

"Get your stuff from my trash, if you decide to even get it," she says. The door closes on me with a slam. Dirt and a candy wrapper fly against my cut jeans.

The Dalmatian drives off with a screech that burns rubber. The smell hits me, and a whine slides out like smooth silk. I open my eyes in time to see the last of her tire smoke, but more importantly, I find blood decorating my newly lightened coat of fur. The dancing rosettes have only grown darker with the faint hint of red.

Not only have I become the victim, but I've just become the bitch.

***

Just like she'd promised, my stuff decorates her front garbage bins like bits of piñata streamers and deflated toys. Not only had she decided to leave it for me, but she'd torn my clothes up, obviously reacting harshly to me calling her out for the bite.

I get back to my apartment, clothes stuffed in used garbage bags, to find the mail spewing out the front door. I've only been gone for a night, two at most, and both my mind and body feel as though they've been thrown through the ringer. It makes sense my house would feel the same way.

"Women," I grumble, and slide my key into the lock. The door slides open, taking the mail with it, and I sniff the air in feigned curiosity.

It smells different, alien almost. Whoever had been here days before surely wasn't the same dog that now stands here waiting, I think. Without wanting to, I cough and feel my stomach wretch within my gut. Seeing it all before my newly black and white muzzle is even more horrifying than I'd imagined. The instincts inside beg to begin a new attempt at marking what'll surely smell like the common dog.

With Samantha gone, the only thing I can do is struggle forward. Maybe go back to the club, accept what's come to me. With a glance, I find that my paws, which have gone from wild, desert-made paws to those of the common canine, are much neater, cleaner now. Again, the clothes I had before now cease to fit on my new runner-frame of muscle

Would it really be that bad? To shift into something new, live a more athletic life, and be taken in as some symbol of patriot honor? What if I did find someone else that suited me, the old me? Then, things would maybe work out as they'd need to.

I step my way indoors, ignoring the old smell that's burying my tail between my legs. When I reach the kitchen, I open the fridge and grab a beer, not even waiting to pop open the cap and drink myself raw.

A wave floods over me unlike anything I've experienced before. My vision sparkles and swims. My legs feel nice and limber. I open another beer, down that one out as well, and find myself smiling under the warmth taking my mind.

At least becoming a dog means that I can finally get drunk.

***

I'm wiping the counter down as the last of the chairs get filled and the lights dim to a warm glow. Already, the band's ended their warm-ups, bass strings tuned and drums tightened. It's a full house, with the audience mostly made up of animals holding their cutie's paws. My lips pull to a smile at the sound of murmurs echoing through the house.

And then they start. The trumpets blare above the staccato of the drummer's beat. I feel the trombone's wash over me with sweet, warm tone. The bar comes to life with solid and jazzy cheers.

Everyone bobs and nods as the song picks up to a ragtime tempo. It's like something's taken over them and erased who they were. All that matters is the jazz. Around the house, different animals share each other's company. I notice a wolf who seems to be shifting towards something feline. His ears perk higher, muzzle sporting heavy whiskers. And then, a gazelle sporting the eyes of a horse. All people who don't seem to care that who they're with is slowly changing them into something new. They're in love. That's what matters.

"Can I get a beer?"

"Bar's closed," I say. "Enjoy the show."

"It's not for me," the woman says. I turn with a lowered brow, until I find an African Wild Dog standing and smiling. Her eyes reflect something I haven't seen in months, haven't seen since...

"Samantha?"

She raises her paws as if caught amidst a crime scene. "Do I get my beer if I know you?"

"You're...how're you..." I stumble and bite my words back, trying to form a question I dare not ask.

"It appears that I wasn't the only one with vicious bites. Took longer than you, I'm sure."

"When did it start?"

"A month ago. It hit me like the flu, and I had to miss work for a few days."

"Work? You work?" I hold myself from barking a laugh. Already, eyes are starting to look our way.

"Shut up. I see you finally decided to stay here. They give you this job because they felt bad for you, or...?"

"I asked for it. Couldn't leave it behind." I nod towards the stage.

"Right," she says.

We're standing there motionless, lost in each other's eyes as the music comes to an end at the first movement. Applause brings us back, and we snap, bubbles burst and returning us to the reality we're stuck in.

"Beer, you said?"

She nods. "Just one."

I grab one of the good ones from down below. With a pop, the cap comes off, and suds flow down my paws and onto the rubber mats we've got stacked on the floor.

When I look up, I find that she's gone. The band's getting ready for the next set, but left on the counter is a five and a small sliver of paper. I take the bill and read the note.

Enjoy the beer. See you after the show. Her number follows with a pair of African Wild Dog ears drawn on like radars.

I laugh as the next number starts and paws begin to clap. With an attitude like hers, who says dogs can't look up?

Good Boy

Friday Donnelly

I shouldn't have cheated on him.

I didn't mean anything by it; I was drunk, the other guy was hot. Well, and he was drunk too. It was a small party, things got touchy, then more. I hadn't really been in that sort of environment before and I didn't really expect myself to feel the ways I did, but I did, and I wish I hadn't.

It's not that I don't love John, I do, I do with all my heart. He's such a funny guy, smart, attractive, and despite the things he says you can tell he genuinely *cares* in a way that makes even the toughest heart melt. You can tell it about him almost immediately. It's fascinating watching people open up to him within a few minutes of meeting him. It's like nothing I've ever seen.

And I do love him too! I wouldn't dream of being with anyone besides him. My judgment was compromised, and I don't know how to tell him without destroying his heart like a dry biscuit crumbling through my grasp. He trusted me.

I won't go into the full details; he's got a kinky side, we were at a gear party, it was my first time, there was some alcohol involved. One of the guys there, I don't even remember his name, was decked out all in leather, harness, jock, cuffs, you name it. He had such a commanding presence and I just… I listened. He wanted me and I was half hot for him, half just so flattered that he would want anything to do with me that after everyone else was sleeping off their drinks and he fit a collar around my neck… I just couldn't help it. I did anything he silently pushed me to do, all while trying to keep the idea of what I was doing to John at the back of my mind even as it threatened every moment to surface.

I'm making a lot of excuses, and I know it. And there were a lot of things that made the situation more excusable. It's true. But at the same time, I was a piece of dogshit and I'm trying to find some way to live with myself about this whole thing.

So what's my plan for now? Well, tell him. He'll be back any moment, and here I am sitting cross-legged on the couch and trying not to cry. He'll know by my face that something's wrong the moment he walks in. It's been a couple days and he already knows something is up anyways; he's like that.

Ah. A car door slamming. Could be anyone's here at this apartment complex, but something inside me knows it's him. The boots stomping up the stairs, the lock turning with a key, the door opening. A bearded face with big stupid earmuffs, cheeks red from the cold, a jacket zipped around a barrel-shaped body, a smile surrounded by long brown hair. God, I love him.

He knows immediately, his eyes concerned. "Honey?"

"I cheated on you." I don't know how to do anything other than blurt it out. I can't take it anymore.

There's a long moment of staring. His gaze is shocked. Mine is awkward. I drop it after a moment, the coffee table's pattern of wear and tear suddenly intensely interesting.

A thump as he drops his coat on the line of shoes; a couple bumping sounds as he lines his boots up next to the other shoes.

"Was it Terrence?" He asks simply.

"The guy at the party. The man in leather. Harness. Thing." It's hard to make sentences more than one word, and harder to make them anything substantive.

He doesn't say anything else. Just walks by the sofa to our room and I hear the door close. I try to choke out a selfish "I love you" as he passes; I don't know if he hears or cares.

A few hours later and I hear the door open. My heart immediately leaps into a full gallop like a racehorse from a starting gate. It's here. The Talk.

John sits down across from me on the recliner, still wearing his business clothes. His giant hairy hands are knit together and after gazing at them for a moment, he looks up at me.

"Why?"

"I was drunk and he was hot and the leather was... I didn't know I liked it so much, I really didn't."

"We could have shared that," he says, hurt. And he's right, and that hurts.

"I know. We can. I just, it caught me by surprise, and he liked me, and..."

"And you liked him."

"... Yes. Not like I like you, it was just... it's different. I don't know how or why, and it sucks, and it's confusing, and it hurts you, and..."

"You like him more?"

I shake my head furiously. "No." And there's conviction in my voice for the first time. I hope he hears it. That is the truth.

He juts his chin out slightly, an almost-nod. "I see."

"He's just a different sort of hot, and you make me feel like I'm everything to you. He made me feel like I was nothing to him. I... like both of those things. I didn't know, and I still don't get how I do, but that's the way, and..."

He silences me with a shake of his hand. "Normal submissive things to feel. Not an excuse to act on them. Condom?"

I shake my head. "Didn't go that way."

He sighs. "Well could be worse I guess."

There's a few minutes of silence. Then he stands and picks up his coat slowly. "I've got to go. I'll be back, I guess."

"Okay," I croak, my voice suddenly dry.

And the door slams and he's gone.

The time passes in a numb quietness. I don't feel like I deserve anything to take my mind off what I've done, so I stare at the ceiling and wonder if this is the end of things, if we're gonna be roommates who share a bed now. If even that is generous, if I'm going to be kicked out. He wouldn't be out of line to demand it even if we're both on the lease.

That car door slamming rings out again; dozens have closed in the past however long it's been, but I know that one.

John walks in with several plastic bags under his arms. He throws them into the center of the room and hangs up his jacket, takes off his boots.

"What's this?" I ask.

He pulls out a giant dog bed and drags it back into our room.

I try again. "John? What's going on?"

He fills a metal water bowl at the sink, places it on a small mat in the corner. An empty ceramic food bowl is set beside it.

Two large bags of dog food end up in the closet, and a couple simple toys are placed on the top shelf of the coat closet. A large kennel is drug into the bedroom, then snapped together with clasps.

"Are we getting a dog?" I ask nervously. It's not something we'd seriously discussed before.

"I am," he says, pulling a wooden box from his pocket. He opens it, and inside is a thick leather collar. A bone-shaped name tag dangles in shiny metal from it. "Roxxie." His pet name for me. I can't help but feel a sudden flush of excitement.

He fastens it around my neck easily; I don't put up a fight. I want to cry. How do I deserve him?

At first all seems okay. I'm so distracted with my feelings and my emotions that the itchiness slowly spreading from my neck doesn't really register–it's there, but just below the surface of my thoughts. It's not until I'm digging my finger under the collar and feel the oddly dry and scratchy skin there that I realize. His hands are holding my face as he stares into my eyes, and I try to say something. "Uh, John, I think I might be allergic or–"

"Quiet, boy. I'm sorry, but I can't let you hurt me like this again. And you'll enjoy it, I know you will," he says.

"No rurry—"

I try to make another sound, to say anything, but it doesn't come out right. Words are failing me, dying in my throat, coming out as garbled growls. Panic rises. If it's causing my throat to swell, my breathing might fail but… it doesn't, even in my panic as I start to hyperventilate with dry, heaving breaths, I can still feel air flowing even if the oxygen doesn't seem to be doing anything.

"Shhh, it's alright boy." John's words flow through my ears and soothe me down to the core as his big arms wrap around my head, holding me close. The itchiness is spreading along my neck and up across my chin like a day without shaving. I scratch and oddly enough, it does feel like I've got a full beard going. As my hands explore up my face, I begin to understand, feeling the hair expanding up my cheeks and growing under my fingertips, pricking them gently, tickling. A quick feel down my neck confirms. I'm growing hair all over my head.

I try to speak again, but once more it's just strangled growls. In frustration, I try to shout. "Bark!"

My cheeks flush of their own accord, under the hair. It can't be.

The changes sweep up the sides of my face and I can feel my ears tugged into tall points. My nose feels congested for a moment, and then it begins to push out, a long, dark brown muzzle slowly creeping forward from my field of vision. I shake my head a little, and it tracks with me, staying resolutely in front. I start, trying to leap from John's grasp, but he holds me tight.

The collar! I reach up to try to pry it off, but my fingers are suddenly so clumsy. Fine motor control disappears as my skull slowly reshapes into a dog's, and my brain with it. Thoughts are difficult, and the words John speaks resonate with my understanding but don't make sense.

The rest of the process feels quick as my torso compacts, barreling out in the front to form a classic German Shepherd's build. My hands contract into themselves and form simple paws, club-like almost, nails elongating and darkening. As master pets me, my butt starts to wiggle and a tail slowly wags its way out, pushing away my pants.

"Here's, let's help you out of these. You don't need them anymore."

And with that, he tugs my shirt off and my clothes fall to the floor. I still feel clothed, a thick layer of fur covering my body, but I whine at the uncertain world around me.

His big hand covers my head as he slowly strokes. "There there, boy. It's alright. You're gonna be taken care of."

The words mean nothing, but the tone is soft, soothing. And his hand is so warm and gentle. I lay down on his lap, waiting, hoping that all this scariness will disappear.

The doorbell rings. Before I know it I'm out of his lap and barking at the door.

"Calm down. It's your friend, Terrence."

Terrence? That word means something. A face, the smell of leather. Good feelings. I sit and wait.

The door opens and it's him, the muscular fellow hugging John and taking off his black leather coat, smiling, kissing him.

I bark, jump up. That's my master! Why is he doing that?

"Down boy," Terrence says, and I fall to my haunches.

"Good boy!" And a treat follows, something savory and meaty. I whine slightly, still unsure. Why was I angry at him? I like Terrence!

"So he's trained?" he asks John.

"Seems like he came from the shelter that way, yeah," John replies.

"That's nice. He seems well-tempered."

"Yeah."

"Sorry about Roscoe," he says. "I thought you guys were open, I really did, we were before so I thought, and I should have asked—"

John cuts him off. "He should have told you."

A curt nod from Terrence. "Yeah. Well I understand asking me for this. I've done the breakup fuck around loop a couple times. I've missed you."

John doesn't say anything, just pushes him against the wall and starts to kiss again. I bark, jump up. That's my master!

"I'll put him in the cage," John says. "I guess that'll be something to train out of him."

A big hand on the back of my collar tugs me to the bedroom. I don't want to. Then a treat's in front of my nose and it smells so good, and next thing I know I'm eating it and the cage door closes with a clank.

John and Terrence kiss for a little while more, their breathing getting heavy. I scratch at the cage door, whine.

"Shh," John says, staring directly into my eyes.

And suddenly everything seems to fall apart. My stomach feels heavy and I lay down, watching as Terrence pulls John's shirt off and the two start to roam each other's body with their hands.

"You've gotten bigger," John murmurs.

"You're kind," Terrence chuckles, taking one of the big man's nipples in his mouth and sucking. His hands tug John's butt, pulling them towards the bed, and John topples on top of Terrence and they keep kissing. I can see everything. I don't want to, but even if I closed my eyes I'd still smell the scent of precum wafting through my cage, the smell of sweaty men and the sounds of grunting and sighing, the occasional gasp. So I watch, feeling my own arousal growing even as I can barely stop myself from whining.

Master.

Terrence.

Not me.

And they're naked, wrestling about, doing things that I should be doing with them, but I can't, and Terrence doesn't even know I'm here, doesn't know who I am.

They're fucking, John on top, Terrence's legs wrapped around him as he's driven into the bed with angry, aggressive thrusts.

A gasp, a few moans. The pacing slows, stops. They stare into each other's eyes in the dark bedroom for a few moments, and I know I'm entirely forgotten.

I whine and scratch at the cage door. John has to let me out, has to let me be… something, again. I can't remember what.

"Not right now, boy," John says with exhaustion. He turns to Terrence. "Take a shower and I'll let him out after. He can sleep on the bed tonight, I guess. The more the merrier."

A few minutes later and Terrence returns, dripping, lets the towel fall. He smells so good as he opens my cage. I make a beeline to John, whining. How could he?

He hugs me, rubbing my chest gently, murmuring softly to me. And as Terrence sits on the edge of the bed, John leans in and whispers the last thing I understand:

"Good boy."

Never Lick A PCV Vixen

Tarl "Voice" Hoch

"God damn it, Kaiya!"

"I was doing what you wanted me to!" My ears flattened.

Sophia stabbed a stubby finger at me in response. "I showed you the video, this was supposed to be something we could share together. And now… now…" The rabbit's ears lowered while she pulled herself from my bed, the tangled sheets we had been intertwined in moments before sliding off her grey pelt. I started to rise, but ended up hugging my knees instead, letting the brown curls of my hair fall around me to isolate me from the world. She was hard to talk to when she got like this.

I watched Sophia leave my bedroom, the roll of her pert ass, so unlike my rounded tanuki rear. Her upturned white tail now nothing more than a bitter longing where before it had called for me to grab it, to run my paw pads along the gentle cleft to dip below—I shook my head. The rabbit shoved the noren curtain covering my doorway aside in a huff.

Letting out a sigh, I let myself fall sideways from my sitting position, still holding my legs. Was this it? After a year, had we finally reached the breaking point? I squeezed my eyes shut, fighting back the tears that lingered there. I tried, I really tried! Was this how it ended?

The sounds of cupboards being opened and closed in quick, sharp movements reached my rounded ears. It still amazed me just how Sophia still hadn't learned the layout of my apartment. Normally she would keep asking me where things were over and over again instead of actually trying to learn their locations. Maybe it was a warning flag like my mother had said.

Sophia was so excited to show it to me when I opened my front door to let her in. We usually didn't get together during a weekday as both of us work jobs with a significant amount of overtime, but when she had called me, Sophia sounded more excited than I'd heard her be over the last year of us dating. How could I say no?

Sophia had slid the DVD into my ancient player. She beamed with so much energy, her foot tapping a quick beat on the woven mat that covered my floor. Inwardly I worried that the vixen below me would thump on her ceiling again, but held my tongue for fear of breaking whatever was causing my girlfriend's excitement.

The rabbit had plopped down beside where I was sitting on my tiny couch, took the remote and pressed play. I had leaned forward, even as Sophia snuggled closer, like she as trying to push her excitement through her skin and fur using osmosis, willing me to share her excitement. The DVD logo came on, and then the title.

Forcible Rough Examination of Tiny Schoolgirl

The video… It had been weird. Or at least weird to me. Like most erotic videos in Japan, things were blurred, but the mosaics were tight and left little to the imagination. I suspected Sophia chose it for that very reason. Scene after scene of women forced against walls, shoved face first into mattresses, and in once case, a model tied up with vibrators placed all over her body set on high before being manhandled by a group of men. I knew Sophia liked things rough, but this… this was all the reasons I preferred women to men. Men were just so… violent.

That's when she started kissing me.

I don't know why I kissed her back. Because it was expected? Because I was shell shocked from the video? Regardless, my body responded to her and soon our hands started travelling over each other's bodies. My paw pads brushed across her smaller chest, strumming the erect bumps of her nipples with each pass. Her paw found my neck, the other trailing down my back to caress near the base of my tail.

I moaned into her shorter muzzle. She leaned back, pulling me with her. Her claws dug into my back while she ground her hips against me, struggling to widen her legs, only to find that I had them trapped. It was her turn to moan. One of my paws squeezed her breast gently, only to have her moan for me to do it harder. When I did, she gasped, her paws moving to my ass, pulling my hips against hers. Her kisses were hungry now, which should have tipped me off, but I was caught up with the familiarity of our movements. When one of her paws moved between my legs, it was a rough push rather than tender caress and I gasped, ears flicking upright.

Her next touch was softer, a gentle slide along my labia even though my panties and yoga pants were in the way. My ears splayed, a sigh escaped me. She grinned when I pulled away from our kiss and I fell in love with her again. One look at that buck toothed lopsided grin. Like a rogue in the night, full of devil may care attitude. Her next words made me giggle.

"Where do you want me?"

My gaze moved from the entrance to my room and then back to her, wondering why she was being like this. Her paws caressed her breasts before travelling down her flat stomach, making things low in me clench, so I nodded towards my room, not trusting my voice. Sophia's grin widened. We were a mad scramble to my bedroom. I stubbed my shin on the table edge of the kotatsu, but that didn't even slow me down. My blood was singing, things low in my body relaxing and shifting. I wanted to touch Sophia again, more so as her tail flagged and drew my gaze to the cleft of her ass. My longer nose could smell her arousal and my nipples tightened at the scent.

I barreled through my bedroom door, pushing the noren aside, stumbling and tripping. I caught Sophia while she was pulling her shirt off and we tumbled to the bed. I took advantage of the fact that her arms and head were trapped in her shirt by kissing and licking along her collar bone, ribs, breasts and finally nipples. The rabbit squirmed, her thighs rubbing together as she tried to fight the shirt.

I grinned and leaned backwards, pulling my own shirt over my head, making sure it didn't get stuck on my muzzle. When I looked down again Sophia had freed herself, but the shirt was still wrapped around her wrists.

A red flag went off in my mind, and I started to say something when she gave me that damned smirk again. I was a moth to flame, muzzle finding hers, tongues pushing and gliding against each other. I ran my paws along her sides, breasts to hips. Unlike my own stockier body, I could feel her ribs where they pressed against her grey pelt. I always envied her ability to stay thin, but I guess that came with being a vegetarian, or so she told me.

The kiss broke, I licked my muzzle while I looked at her. She shivered. Sophia liked that, and I guess now I knew why. She watched, arms still extended above her, while I grabbed the waistband of her shorts and pulled them down, panties and all. Her scent hit me hard, sharp and bitter yet fragrant and heavy. I bent down and in a single lap, traced my tongue along her slit.

Sophia had said something then, and I still couldn't remember what it was. I was concentrating too hard on the way her fur parted to a sweeter wetness inside. Again I licked, and Sophia pushed her hips towards me. But unlike previous times together, this time she kept her arms above her. Did the video really turn her on that much? A flash of the woman who had been shoved face first into a mattress shot across my mind. She had been a squirrel, hadn't she? The way she screamed almost in pain as the wolf had shoved his fingers into her so much I am sure she would have been bruised the next day.

"More, harder!" Sophia's whisper cut through my thoughts. I had been so caught up in the image I had stopped licking her. I looked up at her and saw her staring at me, muzzle partway open, eyes half hooded. Spreading her legs further, her scent wafting up to me to pull my muzzle downwards. Moisture coated her labia, and the taste was heavenly. She moaned and squirmed, pushing herself up towards me with each lap, wriggling back and forth.

Bump.

Her inner thigh caught my cheek, clacking my teeth together and almost catching my tongue. I ignored it and kept licking, alternating between deep strokes where the flat of my tongue pushed her folds apart, to short laps, forcing my tongue's tip between those folds to unfurl inside her.

Bump.

I growled this time, completely by accident, but kept funneling my attention on Sophia. She was getting closer, her lips parting to expose her entrance easier and easier, her tiny clit standing at attention, calling for me to pull it into my lips. And boy did I ever.

Bump.

I grabbed her inner thighs and forced her legs further apart. She moaned loud enough I thought the vixen downstairs would be hitting her roof with a broom again. I forced my tongue into her, harder this time. There are advantages to being a canine, long tongues being one of the best. (Well, except drinking from glasses that is.)

A shiver went through Sophia and her hips bucked. My tongue tingled while her body clamped down on the fleshy intruder, pulling it deeper. As far as orgasms went, this was a small one, and almost as soon as it started, it was over and Sophia was looking down her body at me. The look in her eyes... she wanted something, but I didn't know what. Usually at this point she would pounce me and bring me to as close as a climax as I could get before I would finish her off and we would come together.

So I moved up her body, smiling at her the whole way. I traced my paw pads along her legs, teasing the bend of her knee before caressing her inner thigh. She frowned at me for a moment, until my paw caressed along her slit, my fingers splaying to trace along either side of her clit. She moaned, one leg thumping on the bed for a moment until my fingers continued on. I smiled, she always did love it when I did that.

Moving to straddle her, I placed my own slit near hers. Maybe she wanted to scissor? The sheets were already starting to get tangled around us but I thought it gave her an erotic look, like Venus from the old statues I had seen in a history book. I pushed down on her a bit with my hips. Scissoring wasn't really my thing, but it usually got her off so I was all up for it. Instead, her frown deepened.

"What is it?" I leaned in so that our breasts touched, nipples brushing against each other.

"Really?" She tried to sit up, forcing me to retreat down her body. "You don't know what is wrong?"

I cocked my head to the side, ears raising. "I thought this was what you wanted to do…to make love." I hated how weak my voice sounded.

Sophia rolled her eyes and started to get up.

"God damn it, Kaiya!"

***

"And well, now you know the rest."

The young vulpine seated across from me let his muzzle fall open. "She walked out on you? Just like that? What a bitch!"

"It's just one of her moods, Seiichi." I took a lap at my tea, wincing at how hot it remained despite the cooling air. "You know how she is."

The fox's ears lowered the same time his golden eyes rolled. He pushed the bangs of his asymmetrically cut dyed-blonde hair out of his eyes. Sophia had mentioned once that a lot of people considered the foxes of our country to be super feminine, and with that one gesture, Seiichi proved them all right. "Sure, sure, Kaiya. Just like all the other times she's pulled this shit with you. One moment she's all hot and bothered, the next she's some high and mighty bitch queen. Didn't I warn you not to date an American?"

My own ears lowered a fraction. "Don't be like that Seiichi. Sophia's been good for me."

Seiichi rolled his glass of avocado shake between his paw pads, beads of moisture wetting them. "How long have we been doing these little get-togethers so you could unload your juicy sexual adventures on me?"

That caught me off guard, and I tried to hide my discomfort by taking another couple laps at my tea, burned tongue or not. He watched me, a slow smile creeping across his muzzle. My gaze roamed the small tea shop we had stopped at, admiring the pictures of various foods and drinks available, either from the vending machines or from the few staff on hand, but in the end I had to say something. "I don't know, four or five years?"

The rolling shake stopped and he waved it at me before taking a lap of the cool green sludge. "Exactly. You're the only person I can talk this shit with Kaiya. I am willing to bet that no one here even knows what a clit is." He slow-turned his head to give a wide grin to an older akita couple seated near us who had been stealing glances at us. Their ears flagged up before they raised their paws to block their eyes from his stare. Seiichi remained staring at them a moment longer before turning back to me. "I've listened to your escapades for years. And I have learned a thing or two from listening to you tell me what happens between your sheets."

"That you're a pervert?" I whispered.

He barked out a laugh. "Well, besides that. Maybe if I could actually have some decent rough sex I wouldn't have to rely on your vanilla adventures to lock away in my spank bank for later."

Despite the face I gave him showing my disgust, my tail nub wagged behind me. "Glad I could be of some service."

"What I am trying to say Kaiya, is that I have known you a long time. I cherish these meetings, sexy stories aside. It gives me a chance to vent about my own problems to someone who isn't part of the gay scene so I don't have to worry about it getting around. I can also talk freely, which as mentioned, is huge for me. But one thing our talks gives me are certain insights into you and your personality, and you my dear, aren't kinky."

My ears flashed upwards and then splayed like a badly tuned set of rabbit ears on an old TV. "What?"

Seiichi's grin widened, showing a lot of his teeth. "You aren't kinky, Kaiya. And most certainly not as kinky as me, as I tend to like a lot of abuse and questionable consent shit. But yeah, I can say with some authority you just don't have it, princess."

"So?"

"That's why Sophia was so pissed off. She comes over all hot and bothered with some porn tape filled to the brim with…?"

"Men abusing women."

Seiichi sighed, resting his forehead against the cool glass of his drink. "No. Trust me, that wasn't abuse. Well, it can be, but it isn't." He waved his paws in the air. "It was a video of men dominating women. There was no abusing taking place, at least I hope so anyway. Sometimes with porn idols it's a bit hard to differentiate sometimes… I once saw a video with—"

I growled.

"Right, right," He said. "The point is: all these women were being dominated by these men. Be it shoved into a pillow, gang banged, or whatever, they all are shots aimed at one thing. The fact that Sophia showed this to you means that she wanted you to hopefully catch the hint and do these kinds of things to her."

I sunk lower in my chair. "Is that why I didn't like it?"

He sat up, ears raised, tail wagging behind him. "Sort of. It probably had more to do with you not liking dudes all that much."

It was my turn to roll my eyes. "Then explain the fact that I have had sex with dudes, genius." I took another lap of my tea.

"I betcha it wasn't like that video, was it?"

I coughed, the tea going down the wrong hole. My first thought was of Kenshin and our time together. It had been slow, soft, and touching. It had been exactly how I wanted to lose my virginity and nothing like some of the stories other girls whispered about in the locker room at school. My ears were burning when I finally met Seiichi's gaze and he leaned back, laughing. More than one of the older patrons at the teashop shot us annoyed looks, making me sink lower in my chair, ears flattening.

"See what I am talking about though?" The fox said when he

finally leaned forward to take another lap at his shake. "Couple that with your aversion to a good ol' fuck—"

More glares from the other patrons and I was wishing I had brought my hoodie with me so I could have hidden in the hood's depths. The couple that Seiichi had grinned at got up with a huff, the man muttering something while his date stole a long glance over her shoulder at us as they left.

"—and now you see why Sophia was so miffed."

My voice was a whisper. "So you're saying she wanted me to be like those guys?"

Seiichi sighed, resting his head on both his paws. His ears splayed out and he got a far away look in his eyes. "Oh fuck did she ever. She wanted you to take her, shove her down, tell her to bite the pillow and use all those freaky dildos you have on her as roughly as possible until she was a quivering mess."

My ears felt like they were on fire and when I went to take a lap of my tea I found I had emptied not only my bowl, but also the tea pot. "Seriously?" I managed to squeak out.

The fox's expression told me he was lost in some internal fantasy where he was no doubt in the position that Sophia had probably wanted to be in. I couldn't believe I had been so blind, so ignorant. But then why? Why had she wanted me to do these things to her? She knew what I liked, what I was comfortable with. Hell, we'd had talks about my opinions of guys and the whole penis centric view of sex. There was no way…

I sat up and leaned in close to Seiichi. "But she's a woman, and we're not like that! Men are all rough and tumble. Women are the neat ones, the restrained ones, the delicate flowers."

The vulpine reached out and tapped my nose with a slender finger. "Have you ever talked about sex with each other?"

I shook my head, sinking back into my chair and closing my eyes, letting my breath out in a long sigh. "No, we haven't. It's never felt like a good time."

With one last tap on the end of my muzzle, Seiichi leaned back.

"And there is problem number one. Not all women are delicate flowers, and American women… well, let me put it this way. You ever seen American porn?"

I shook my head.

"Here in Japan, we have some freaky shit. But those Americans… damn. They're freaky."

I whined, ears sinking.

"Don't act like it's the end of the world, Kaiya."

"Why didn't she just come out and ask me?"

He shrugged in response. "Maybe it's embarrassing for her? Sometimes it's easier to show than to simply ask? Or maybe she thought this way it would be more… natural?" He brushed his hair out of his eyes again. "You're the one that said you haven't really talked about sex, remember?"

"But how am I supposed to do that for her? Look at how hard of a time you're having finding someone to do that stuff with you!"

Seiichi looked up at the sky. "Sure, I come to you for sexy stories because my own sex life sucks. And sure, I can't really find someone who will dominate me quite in that perfectly 'won't take no for an answer' rough and tumble sort of manner, but that doesn't mean you can't at least fulfill Sophia's fantasy…" His gaze snapped down. "Even if she is a bitch."

"Not this again." I grumbled, standing up and placing a few 500 Yen coins on the table for our drinks while Seiichi used his long tongue to get every last drop of avocado out of his milkshake glass. *If only he liked girls…*

"Hey," he managed to say between licks, "I just call them like I see them. This is only going to get worse." He finished the glass and stood. Giving me a flourished bow like some kind of prince would, he jerked his thumb down the street. "What did you want to do today?"

My ears jumped and my tiny tail nub wagged. "Shopping?"

The vulpine laughed as he took my arm and led me down the street. "Now tell me, what would you have done to Sophia knowing what you do now…?"

***

"Uuuhhh, are you sure about this?"

Seiichi glanced over his shoulder and grinned at me. "I've been here a couple times before. Yoshimura has some pretty interesting stuff."

I looked around at the shelves. Whoever this Yoshimura was, he sure loved…stuff. The store was small and cramped, metal shelves that looked like they had been stolen from a medical clinic covered most of the store. I saw old Gundam models I swear were worth hundreds of dollars to collectors sharing shelf space with glass jars filled with various herbs and less identifiable things. The entire store smelled like an Egyptian mummifying chamber—not that I knew what that smelled like. More than once I had to cover my nose with the inside of my elbow to stifle my sneeze.

"Look at this!" Seiichi's arm shot out from behind one of the metal shelves. My eyes widened.

"That's, that's…!"

Seiichi's face appeared from around the shelf, his smile all teeth. "The Sassy Princess Rock It Nude 1/6 scale PVC figure with optional blindfold? Still in its packaging? Hell yeah!"

I was down the hallway of shelves like a ninja across a moonlight cityscape. Seiichi's ears stood straight up as I snatched it out of his paws, almost taking his arm with the PVC figure. I rotated the box, checking it over for the smallest flaw. My nose was almost pressed against the packaging, my sense of smell working overtime but not getting much other than the scents of the shop. The packaging was in near-perfect condition. The figure-

My gaze travelled over the spread legs of the vixen inside. She was sprawled out on her back to expose massive breasts, the elegant curve of her arched back, her bent legs parted to expose… my gaze moved to the price, my heart threatening to burst and things low in my body starting to dampen my panties. I knew how much this figure cost on eBay. Forty thousand Yen would put a nice amount of frigid water on my hormones.

"Wait, what?" I looked from the price tag to Seiichi's grinning face. "You're kidding me."

Leaning in, his muzzle was almost against my ears. "The thing with Yoshimura is that he often doesn't know what market values are for the product he sells, often selling them near or slightly above cost," he whispered. Pulling back, Seiichi winked at me before vanishing once again among the shelves.

"But thirteen thousand yen? That's more than half the price…" My lungs felt out of breath, my words a ghost gone in moments. I clutched the figure to my chest, careful not to mar the box.

I wandered through the rest of the store, gaze hunting for any more figures among the elective items there. I saw a few, but when my eyes made their way to the price tags, I found that they were priced much closer to eBay than the prize clutched to my chest.

When I reached the back corner of the store, I found Seiichi standing in front of a counter with a paper bag already hanging from a paw. He shifted to the side, glancing at me before going back to talk to Yoshimura. Or at least I assumed it was him until I got closer and Seiichi introduced me to the middle aged shiba inu.

"Nice to meet you, young lady," Yoshimura said, bowing slightly to me once introductions were finished. "It's nice to see Seiichi has such a friend as you. For a while there I thought he was *dōseiaisha*, but with someone as pretty as you at his side, I am glad to know I was wrong." He turned to my friend. "My apologies, Seiichi."

I cocked my head to the side while Seiichi scratched the back of his head with one paw. "It's nothing Yoshimura, that's one reason I brought Kaiya over to meet you. Well, that and she is a huge fan of some of the stuff in your shop, just like I am."

"Is this true young lady?" Yoshimura smiled at me.

I placed my find on his desk and he bent down to carefully study it. Making a small chuff noise, quick fingers punched up the price on an ancient cash registrar. Its ding made me jump.

"I see you have the same weird tastes as your vulpine friend here, but don't worry, I won't judge you. Everyone has to have a hobby, don't they? I hear there's quite the community for these figures."

I smiled and nodded, not sure what to say while he carefully placed the packaged figure into a paper bag and handed it to me. A small thank you made it out of me which made the older canine smile.

"I will have to keep ordering in more of these figures then, if it brings around such a beautiful creature such as yourself."

I toed the floor until Seiichi took my arm and steered me towards the door. "Thanks again Yoshimura! I'll be sure to bring her back to visit next time!"

The shiba inu waved at us before we put some of the racking between us. His voice sounded distant. "Anytime Seiichi! She is a cute girlfriend, treat her right!"

***

We had just stepped off the train and were waiting to cross the street away from the station when I finally got the nerve to mention what Yoshimura had said to Seiichi. "Yoshimura doesn't know you're gay?"

The vulpine looked sideways at me, his ears moving up and down before splaying slightly. "I suspected he thought I was. He's an open-minded guy, except when it comes to penises in butts." He let out a laugh. "I'm sorry to kinda use you like that, but this way he won't harass me about having a girlfriend or never seeing me with anyone other than guys. Plus, I knew you'd like his store. I usually find a few treasures there anytime I go." He looked down in his own paper bag. I caught a glimpse of a few things, including a couple of the herb filled glass jars marked with those weird magic symbols I had seen in the latest magical girl anime. I almost asked him about them, but held my tongue. It wasn't my place to pry.

"Doesn't it bug you though?"

Seiichi shrugged, looking sideways at me. "Not really. I've been up against stuff like this for a very long time. You do what you can, pick your battles and sometimes you just have to let it go."

"See, that's what I am doing with Sophia."

He turned to face me with a snort. "Nice try, Kaiya, but it doesn't work like that. The difference between what we're doing is that you're being taken advantage of, and she's trying to mold you into her perfect sex machine for *her* needs. Not yours."

"But—"

"Listen Kaiya, Sophia is used to getting what she wants. It was how she was raised, the society she is a part of, and that doesn't fly over here. Instead of trying to adapt to another culture, she's barging her way through it and doing the same to your relationship." The light changed to a walk signal and both of us started across the street, Seiichi continuing to talk.

"I don't want to see you hurt. Listening to your sex lives is thrilling to me, sure, but it seems hardly healthy from where I stand. You're going to either have to find a way to get what you both want, or one of you is going to break."

We reached the other side of the street and continued walking in silence while I looked at the houses and apartments lining the street; anywhere but the fox beside me. When we reached a four way stop beside a small neighborhood market, we stopped and I felt his paw come to rest on my shoulder.

"I like you Kaiya, you're a really good friend. I want you to be happy." A mischievous grin crossed his muzzle. "I want you to have really, really amazing sex."

I laughed, tension leaving my body. "And you want me to tell you about it, right?"

He bowed to me formally. "It would be an honor to listen to your super amazing adventures in the realm of super sexuality." Looking up he flashed me a grin.

"Well maybe one day I will find that person, or maybe Sophia will actually be that person."

"Doubtful." Seiichi turned and headed down the street while I turned down my own.

"Maybe one day you'll end up getting the rough and tumble sex with some massive muscular dude!" I called after him.

He thrust a thumb up into the air. "Toss in a big dick and I am good to go!"

My ears perked as I picked out three distinct windows slamming shut.

It took me two blocks for my giggles to fade.

***

"Careful…," I whispered. "Careful."

I slowly opened the figure's packaging seam by seam, peeling back the sticky transparent circles of tape that held the opening closed. My heart was racing and my ears were burning from standing erect for so long. Yet still I kept at it until I managed to slide the clear plastic protective holder out of the thin cardboard housing. Then carefully I pried it apart and cradled the PVC figure in my paws. I would set the box somewhere safe later on, but now the PVC vixen drew my gaze.

The vixen's bright molded fur stood out against the black of my paw and arm fur, making her more radiant to me. My gaze travelled over her reclining form, taking my time unlike when I had been in the shop. I knew there'd be a wet spot on my bed's comforter when I moved, but there was a reason I was naked.

I caressed the inner thigh of my leg, brushing the fur gently in large circles, slowly moving upwards. Already I could smell my own arousal. It wasn't unappealing. A past girlfriend had said I smelled like sakura petals with a hint of mint. It had made me giggle at the time before her tongue made me make other noises. But for some reason what she had said stuck with me and now I tended to agree with her.

The vixen's body was elegant, even if her breasts were a bit out of proportion for her body, but that just drew the gaze, and with it, my paw moved to my own modest breasts. I traced my areola, plucking at my nipple even as my gaze wandered over the vixen's own pert nubs. I tried to imagine what it would be like to take one of those taut pieces of flesh into my muzzle, to lick it and pluck at it with my front teeth, making the vixen gasp.

Would she do the same to me?

I pinched my nipple between my fingers and let out a gasp.

Things low in my body were fluttering and I ran my free hand down my body, palm flat against my stomach as it travelled over the small belly to dip lower, and lower, and—

I moaned, biting my lower lip, eyes never leaving the small figure held in my other paw. I imagined the fingers tracing my nether lips were hers. The barest tease of blunt claws against the tender softness. The light play of a paw pad against my clit, teasing it to draw forth another gasp.

Oh how I would lay back as the princess explored me, teasing me with tongue, claw and paw. To look up and see those beautiful green eyes staring down at me, knowing she had both a galaxy and rock band to command, and yet have her put it all aside to concentrate solely on me. Sophia would never do something like this for me, would never take her time and explore. Had she ever?

My vision wavered for a moment as my body tightened, the skin under my fur goose-bumping at alien fingers running over my fur. I closed my eyes and sighed, a finger sliding into me, instantly damp before being joined by another.

"Fuck." I moaned.

I fell onto my back, still holding the small figure in front of my muzzle. I lowered it to nose, that delicious valley between the vixen's parted legs. My tongue slid out between my lips and traced across the plastic. I could feel every inch of those bared thighs, the small rise of her vulva, the intricately sculpted labia.

The fingers inside me moved in and out while I continued my ministration to my miniature goddess. The imagined feel of invisible paws continued and I didn't want to stop for fear that I would once again find myself alone in my room. So my free paw moved faster, my fingers arching to rub against a spot Sophia could never seem to find. I was panting in earnest now, my gaze locked on the vixen's half lidded eyes, imagining her breath caressing my ear, ruffling my fur.

My tongue continued to trace over her tiny body, trying to push into places the PVC was not able to yield. I desperately wanted to taste her, to have her cum over my fingers or tongue. Things in me were tightening fast, my vision swimming each time my fingertips pushed deeper. I squeezed my thighs together, trapping my paw between them. I drove hard with my fingers and stared into that miniature vixen's eyes.

The orgasm hit me hard. I forcefully kept my thighs together, even as wetness exploded outwards from me, soaking my fur and the comforter underneath me. I yelled out while I kept my fingers pressed against the softness within me. Wave after wave crashed over me, each drawing out a shuddering spray of liquid until I collapsed.

My room smelled like sakura and mint.

I placed the tiny figure on the pillow beside me before closing my eyes and drifting off.

A vixen's chuckle that changed into something masculine chased me to the comfort of sleep.

***

It was still night when I opened my eyes. Rubbing the back of a paw against them, I slowly sat up, careful to not squish the figure still resting on the spare pillow. I looked at it while I plucked it up. Images of the evening came back to me and my ears burned. It wasn't like I hadn't had fantasies about fictional characters before, but this was the first time I had done something like... *that*.

I sat it on my bedside table and rose, wincing at the way my fur stuck to my comforter. I would have to wash it tomorrow in the tub, it being too heavy for my tiny washer and drier. A quick glance at my clock radio showed it wasn't past midnight yet, though since I didn't have to work or go to school tomorrow, I wasn't too concerned.

Looking back at the figure, I smirked. Seiichi was going to have a field day with this when I told him. Maybe it would prompt him to get some big and muscular figure for himself. The image of the tiny vulpine going down on a PVC figure made me break out in giggles, though it was hard to ignore the warmth that stirred in me.

"That's weird." I mumbled, turning away from the vixen figure in embarrassment. Yet the image of Seiichi going down on a muscular man didn't fade so easily. The bathroom light was painfully bright to me when I flicked it on. I stumbled in while blinking, managing not to stub my toes on anything, and made it to the sink. A splash of cold water chased away the last of my drowsiness and I stepped back. A glance into the mirror made me grin. It looked like I had been through some of the hottest sex in my life.

Too bad it was with myself.

It doesn't have to be. My ears lowered at the masculine voice and I blinked slowly at my reflection.

It doesn't have to be.

Closing my eyes, I splashed more water on my face. "That'll teach me to go down on PVC… probably poisoned myself."

But it was good, wasn't it?

My reflection stared back at me when I met its gaze, nothing having changed. Yet the voice… I glanced through the bathroom door at the floor to ceiling bookshelf creaking under my collection of manga and light novels. I had read about stuff like this before, but those were just—

Stories? Do you know how often you mortals turn to things like that?

I moved out of the bathroom, pinching the bridge of my nose. "This has to be a dream."

Hardly.

"Then what?" My ears flattened, my voice more of a growl.

I felt my gaze being drawn back to the vixen figure. Part of me was still drawn lustfully towards it, though less than before. But another part—it felt revulsion, aversion, a sick feeling in the back of my skull.

I have been trapped in that infernal thing for years. You set me free.

"Who are you?"

I have gone by many names throughout the eras, but Vashruc will suffice.

"And what exactly *are* you?"

A demon.

I laughed.

"Now I know I am dreaming. I've seen enough movies to know a demon would never give out its name, that would give me power over them! Maybe I got some kind of poisoning from the PVC. Maybe that tea had something in it?"

Oh the ignorant. A name is a name, nothing more. The voice laughed in my mind. *Ever since that old shaman dropped the coin I had been inhabiting into the mould for that figure to get rid of me, I have been waiting for someone to come along and release me. And you, young tanuki, are that someone.*

"So what you are saying is: If I get rid of that figure, you'll be out of my mind and body and gone forever?"

If you hadn't opened yourself to me, perhaps that would have worked. But now…

My arm moved of its own accord, my pointer and middle finger splaying into a victory sign. My muzzle opened to scream and my hand clamped it shut.

Now that just won't do now, will it? Do you know how long I have waited to be released from that prison? How many innocents I could have corrupted, could have wrecked, in that time? Ruined them for their future lovers? Ruined them in the eyes of God?

I whimpered, trying to shake away from the iron grip around my muzzle.

You can not imagine how good it feels to have a body again, even if it's female. Perhaps I could seduce a few young boys, take their innocence before they are ripe. Nothing is as sweet as spoiled sweet meat. The voice seemed to search around in my head, a weird buzzing of thoughts and images coming to the forefront of my mind. Suddenly Seiichi's mischievous face came to mind. I remembered that look, it had been when I told him about this new online sex store that sold unusual dildos from the States. I had been describing one modelled off a western dragon and I could feel his lust radiating off him.

What do we have here? More buzzing in my mind. *Seiichi huh? Poor little fellow can't get roughed up in quite the way he wants to, can he? He thinks himself an experienced one it would seem. Well perhaps I should educate him in the sin of Pride.*

The paw holding my muzzle suddenly released, causing me to gasp and pant. "So what of it?"

I have been trapped in that idol for far too long, little one, and I have itches that need to be scratched. I need something to practice on, and he does so look like soft meat.

I laughed. I couldn't help myself. "You said it yourself demon-boy. I'm a girl. Good luck with that!"

The corners of my muzzle lifted into a grin. *Easy enough to fix.*

I doubled over, Vashruc's laughter echoed in my skull. No period cramps had ever felt as bad as what tore through me. Falling to all fours, my muzzle stretched wide in a silent scream as a crawling rolled through me just under my skin. My eyes went wide and I let out a choking bark as my back hunched, each muscle in my body feeling like it was on fire.

"What is wrong with me?"

My stomach cramped again, the feeling shifting through me, spreading along my body. Each muscle along the way flexed and felt like it was going to burst. I gripped my stomach and rested my forehead on the wooden floor. "You've been hung over before Kaiya," I said to myself, gritting my teeth. "This is just like then, only worse. You can ride it out!"

Another wave of cramps stole the thought away to be replaced with the laughter of the demon within me. A crack reverberated off the walls as my jaws widened again, this time something dislocated, pulling it apart. What felt like worms crawled through my mouth and over my muzzle, lengthening and strengthening it. I shut my eyes only to have another crack echo when something in my ribs expanded and broke.

I whimpered, unable to draw breath while I fell to my side. My legs kicked, my hind claws catching the kotatsu and knocking it askew. Raising my paws to my face, I watched as the fingers thickened and lengthened, becoming more like claws than the blunt things I had taken methodical care of every day since I was six. My muzzle snapped shut and I growled, tears starting to stream down my cheeks as the rest of my body started to shift and change. It was like I was on a rack, my limbs being pulled further than they should naturally go. My tailbone was on fire and everything itched as skin and fur stretched and changed.

Something shifted low in my body. I couldn't help but look down to see my clit suddenly surged outwards like a growing vegetable shown in time lapse. My guts turned as veins pulled from me and wrapped themselves around its length moments before fur coated it in a sheath. Heaviness suddenly tugged me downwards and my paw went to them, feeling weighty testicles where my slit had been moments before.

My growl deepened, becoming louder and more threatening. I threw back my head and roared, my shelves rattling, figures of various anime characters clattering to the floor. Immediately my ears picked up the sound of banging on the floor beneath me, the vixen downstairs' muffled yelling quickly following. I surged upwards, coming to my feet and turned. What I saw in the reflection of the patio door had me looking at my massive paws again.

I was a monster.

Gone was my small round little body with its cute curvy booty. I wasn't a tanuki anymore. Instead I was a… a… I raised my gaze back to my reflection. Softly glowing crimson eyes met my gaze from beneath a wild mane of hair the colour of crimson. Thick slabs of muscles covered me, rippling under fur the colour of crematorium ash. I was easily twice, if not three times as large as I had been. I turned, and my body moved with the grace of a hunter, the muscles moving easily under the fur. I opened my muzzle and was greeted with a multitude of pointy teeth that gleamed in the night. Turning, a long furred tail swayed, its shape more akin to a cartoon demon than any beast of this planet.

"What have you done to me?" I snarled at the reflection.

What needed to be done. Vashruc wrenched control from me and flexed into the refection. Turning, the demon flexed again before his tail gave a satisfied wag behind our body. *This way I can scratch my itch a lot easier than in your previous form.*

His paw went to our sheath and cradled it, as if weighing a sack of fruit at the market. Giving a nod he turned to the window. I could feel him sifting through my mind, grabbing any information he could in regards to Seiichi while he snatched a pair of yoga pants from the floor and pulled them on. I pushed against him, screaming in my mind, but moments later he had what he wanted.

Time to pay your friend a visit, little one, let us hope he likes what you've become.

With that, he slid the patio window open and I went out into the night like some kind of anime monster, a prisoner in my own body.

***

Seiichi opened his front door wearing a black robe and blinked up at my—or rather the demon's—body. "Hello?"

My body looked down at him, a smile breaking across my muzzle. Shadows danced around me, hiding me almost from his view. "Hello, little boy."

"Do I know you?" The fox leered up at me, head cocking to the side, ears rising.

I had been preparing for this ever since we left my house. With a snarl I fought against the demon, wrenching against his control, tearing him away for a moment.

"It's me Seiichi! This thing changed my body!"

"Kaiya?"

"That figure, it had a demon in—" A snarl tore itself from my muzzle as the Vashruc wrenched my control away. The shadows cloaking us fled. "Kaiya has shown me what you most desire little boy."

Seiichi yipped, his ears folding back while he fled into his room. *Shut the door!* I mentally screamed. *Shut the door!*

Instead, I followed him in. I could hear the fox's heartbeat, rapid-fire in his chest. The demon grinned, running his paws over my now muscular chest before hooking its clawed thumbs into the waistband of the yoga pants. "She said you were in need of a true man, a powerful man."

Something swelled below, the feeling uncomfortable, yet heavy and satisfying. Seiichi's gaze moved lower to—I mentally gasped as Vashruc looked down. The front of the sweats had grown, a large bulge now filled not only the front of the pants, but also most of the upper thigh of one leg.

"See anything you like?" Vashruc chuckled through my transformed throat.

The vulpine's gaze darted up to meet the demon's eyes and then back down to where the already tight lycra was tenting. "Kaiya, are you really in there? Is that really you?"

Another chuckle from the demon who took a step forward into the room, closing the door behind him with a nudge of his foot. "She's in here, I am part of her now. Her lust called to me, as yours calls to me through your fear. It is… delicious. I have such sights to show you."

The creature's laughter rippled through the small apartment, echoing off the walls and filling the tiny space. Seiichi whimpered, a sound I had never heard him make before. But I could also smell his arousal, the scent fruity yet musky: sandalwood and rose.

Another step forward and Seiichi bumped against one of the

many bookcases in his living room. A quick glance by Vashruc brought laughter from the demon's throat. "You're a sorcerer!"

Indeed, the books on the shelves were a mix of manga and tomes with titles straight out of Harry Otter. Manga figures shared space with the odd skull or religious icon. I hadn't been into his apartment that often, and the few times I had, I had never looked at the books on his shelves, being too preoccupied with telling him whatever tale I had to tell. Seiichi reached behind him to something on the shelf.

In a blur he thrust forward some sort of stone. Runes on its surface flared to life as it came near us, but Vashruc swatted it aside, sending the stone bouncing off the recliner in one corner of the room. The demon grinned, flashing his teeth at the smaller vulpine whose gaze was now definitely locked on my—the demon's—bulge. It was very uncomfortable, and I wanted to reach down and adjust it, like a thong caught between my labia. My body stepped forward until I towered over the smaller fox. His head only came to the lower part of my chest.

I felt… powerful.

"Do you like what you see?" Vashruc asked, reaching out to run his massive paw over Seiichi's head. The fox was shaking, though he still leaned into it, if only slightly. "It has been a long time since I have been under the ministrations of a sorcerer."

Run away! I screamed at my friend, trying to force my voice through the eldritch body, but the demon's hold was solid.

He will not hear you. He is mine as surely as you are.

The demon grabbed a pawful of Seiichi's hair, making the vulpine yip in surprise. He reached up, grabbing my new body's forearm as he tried to pull away.

"You can try, little fox, you can try. But then, if you succeed, how will you know what pleasures I can show you?" The massive paw pulled Seiichi away from the bookshelf and against my new body; against the throbbing thing struggling to get loose within the confines of the sweatpants.

My friend made a high-pitched noise in his throat while trying to pull away from the paw gripping his hair, but his struggles only rubbed him further against my member. Each touch sent a shiver along me, a knife's edge to my nerves. It felt good and I wanted more.

Vashruc smiled down at the small male trapped against our chest, smiling to reveal the multitude of teeth within our jaw. Seiichi looked up, his eyes going wide, his pupils expanding in… awe? The fox whined ears splaying, breath and heartbeat breakneck against my body.

"Why do you resist vulpine? You clearly want this, yet you resist. You stink of lust and need!" The demon's voice rumbled from deep in our barrel chest. The scent of arousal was heady in the air now, mixing with the spice of fear. I wanted to tear my pants off, the discomfort was edging on pain. I wanted to do something, anything, but didn't know where to start. Yet a small part of me was confused. Was this really what Seiichi wanted? Even though I could smell his musk and arousal plain on my nose, he couldn't really want *this*, could he?

Vashruc answered it for me, pushing down on my friend's head, forcing him to his knees.

"You know what I want, slave!"

Seiichi whimpered even as his paws moved up to grasp the elastic of the sweatpants, slowly pulling them downwards, careful to pull them out as they moved over the rampant bulge that lay in waiting. Both Seiichi and I gasped at what freed itself.

I had handled salami's smaller than the beast that stood proud between us now. It looked like an engorged crimson serpent, a size queen's dream. My previous body would have ached in places deep inside itself at one glance, but now I could only feel the sheer weight of the thing. Thick fluid dribbled from its tip to fall heavily to the carpeted floor.

"Suck it."

It was not a request.

Seiichi swallowed before raising his dainty muzzle upwards. He nuzzled along the shaft, his paws moving to gently cradle it, his fingers unable to wrap fully around it. Slowly his tongue poked out, pink against the white of his muzzle.

He paused.

The demon pulled at his hair.

He yelped, a shiver rippling his fur, tail darting for a moment behind him.

The tongue touched the veined flesh and a bolt of pleasure coursed through my body. It was so soft, so warm, as it ran along the underside of my length. This wasn't someone licking at my clit. This was… it was…

Another lick tore a mental gasp from me, but the Vashruc continued to watch, making sure I couldn't turn away from my friend as he slowly broadened his licks, turning them from mere tests of the flesh to full tongue laps.

My body felt like it was laying on a cushion of pins. Each pinprick dancing across my flesh, drawing out shivers of sensation. The demon pulled Seiichi's head away from our member and bent down, baring our teeth as he did. "I said suck it!"

Seiichi's ears dropped and he nodded, looking up at us without raising his muzzle. The demon leaned us back and pulled the fox towards his member. Seiichi swallowed and opened his muzzle as the massive mushroom tip bumped his nose. I shivered at the sensation, but moaned as the tiny fox took the organ into his muzzle.

It felt… it felt… I closed my eyes as he took me in further. No wonder men wanted me to suck their dicks. It was so different than having a woman go down on me. Instead of all the sensations sparking around within me, this was all external. Every movement of his muzzle over the flesh of my member, the way his tongue would glide along its underside, one fleshy muscle pushing against another. Sure, my clit was more sensitive, but there was just so much more area for Seiichi to run his tongue along. Vashruc tightened our grip on Seiichi's hair, pushing our member further into the vulpine's muzzle.

I thought he would choke my friend, but Seiichi managed to get a fair bit in before gagging, pulling back against the demon's paw as his eyes went wide.

Let him go, let him go! He'll choke to death! I screamed at the demon.

Pearls of tears formed in the corner of Seiichi's eyes, and yet the Vashruc held our member in my friend's muzzle. Suddenly his paw released and Seiichi's head flew back, thick ropes of saliva connecting his mouth to the dripping cock before him.

"Very nicely done, little fox," the demon rumbled. "Now get back to it!"

Seiichi was staring at the floor, the movements of his ears the only thing that told me he had heard the demon. Vashruc reached out and grabbed the fox's muzzle, jerking it upwards. Another whimper escaped my friend's throat before the demon brought Seiichi's mouth to our member. Once his maw was released, the fox gave the glistening drop of pre a lick before starting to suck on it in earnest.

We watched him, the demon and I, as his head bobbed up and down on our flesh. He would tilt his head one way and then another, his paws moving to caress the shaft and fondle the heavy balls beneath. It was a weird mix of pleasure and awkwardness. I wanted to shy away, yet wanted more. I had to admit, it was sexy as hell. And when he looked up at us, sheer pleasure rippled through my body. I wanted to grab his head and thrust myself deeper into his muzzle. It was so good!

Vashruc had other ideas, pulling my friend's mouth off us. "Move to the center of the room!"

I was amazed that Seiichi did, eyes ever cast downwards.

"Remove the robe!"

My friend reached up and undid the clasp at his throat. A moment later the robes fell to the floor in a hiss of fabric. Even though his back was to us, I could tell Vashruc loved what he saw. Seiichi was thin like most foxes in this part of the world, his fur glistening in a way mine never did, speaking of hours of brushing. His tail was majestic where it curled around his legs. And his ass. I would have killed for an ass like that, rather than my plump tanuki one.

Vashruc circled him like a shark. It made me feel powerful, more so to see the small pink shaft peeking from my friend's sheath. The thought that he was enjoying this made me want to lick my lips, and I was surprised when our body did the same.

"Every bit as sexy as the girl thought you were."

Seiichi looked up at the demon's words. "You think I'm sexy?"

The backhand rocked his muzzle to the side. It hadn't been hard, just enough to shock him. "She thinks many things about you sorcerer, none of them relevant right now." Stepping forward, the demon's paw went to the back of Seiichi's head and pulled him closer. Our muzzle met his, our tongue forcing its way between his lips and teeth. The kiss was all power, our tongue pushing against his. He responded, more readily than I expected. Our grip on his head tightened, claws digging into the back of his skull and still we pushed ourselves at him, as if Vashruc were trying to devour my friend.

When we broke, the only thing keeping Seiichi standing was our paw. A glance downwards told us he was ready, his member proud and hard. The demon pulled him against us again, and I could feel his cock's heat radiating against my leg. It sent a thrill through me, making my own member throb where it was trapped against the fox's chest.

We took a step forward, Seiichi one backwards. We growled low in our chest and my friend swallowed, raising his muzzle upwards. Our muzzle locked against his throat, teeth pricking the skin there. I could feel his heartbeat as a steady rhythm against my tongue. My free paw slid down his back and grabbed his ass cheek. He squeaked, the sound delicious under our tongue. Another step forward and he relented until he bumped against his recliner. We released his throat, shoving him backwards so he sprawled over the chair's arm.

"I am going to enjoy this," Vashruc said, taking my friend's legs and pulling them so they were fully extended. Stretching them out to the side, I thought he would break the fox like a chicken wing, but it turned out Seiichi was far more flexible than I gave him credit for. His cock stood like a sundial, twitching in quick pulses along with his heart beat.

Releasing one leg, the demon took his glistening member and nudged it against my friend's pucker. Seiichi's eyes widened, then closed as he threw his head back while the demon pushed. I didn't think it would go in, but the heavy amount of pre the demon was producing, as well as Seiichi's saliva seemed to do the trick. With a pop, the fat head pushed through.

Seiichi's eyes remained closed, his breathing controlled, but I could see the way he gripped the fabric of the recliner, the way his ears flicked back and forth, and the way his whiskers pushed forward; he was enjoying himself.

An inch slid in, and then another. Seiichi gasped, his brow furrowing. He was tearing into the upholstery of the chair but didn't seem to notice. Another inch went in and he cried out, his eyes going wide in a moment, meeting our gaze before falling to try and see where we impaled his body.

The demon thrusted and a yelp forced our ears back even as our member went forwards.

I couldn't believe how tight Seiichi was. The feeling was incredible! Warmth surrounded me, engulfed me, cradled me. It was completely different than being filled, having something hot inside me. Despite how rigid my masculine body was, being in Seiichi felt oddly feminine. Even the tightest woman I had been with didn't compare to the way his body hugged the length now inside him. I thought he would burst. It didn't look possible, but with another thrust and a few inches more, and we were almost completely inside the vulpine. I didn't know where he was putting it, but when we finally stopped pushing, stared down at himself as if he didn't believe it either.

"I am impressed sorcerer, very few could take all of my majesty."

Seiichi blinked back his tears and gave a weak laugh. Taking a deep breath, his ears rose and he glanced back, a grin plastered on his muzzle. "I can take a lot." He winked.

The fuck, Seiichi!

Vashruc laughed, grabbing my friend's hips, sliding his cock backwards until it was almost completely out. "Is that so, sorcerer?"

I could almost taste the lust in the look my friend gave us. "Try me."

The first thrust rocked the vulpine against the arm of the chair. The second brought two of the legs off the floor. The third had the fox making high-pitched noises. Fat drops of pre oozed from the fox's member to drip onto his fur, darkening it before slowly sliding along his taut stomach. I was fascinated by it. Compared to the monster that now moved in and out of my friend, Seiichi's cock was a work of art. It was small, but not in the way that leaves women giggling behind their paws. Slender, the shaft rose above its knot in an elegant curve. Moisture seemed to glisten off it like a ripe piece of fruit. If the demon thought of it the same way, I didn't know.

Instead, Vashruc picked up its pace, leaning down over the small vulpine. His paws moved from my friend's hips to his shoulders, and then one to his throat. Seiichi gasped and started to shiver. The demon snarled and he slapped his paw under the fox's jaw, snapping his muzzle shut.

"You will not cum until I do!" Vashruc commanded through clenched teeth.

The thrusts came faster, each one shoving the chair onto two legs and back down, bringing the fox back onto the beast's member. Our breath was getting ragged now, and I could feel something building in me, a pressure not unlike when I was close, only lower. It drove us to thrust deeper, harder, faster.

And then it burst.

With a final thrust, I felt everything release as we threw our head back and roared. The first burst seemed to pulse from my very soul and down my cock and into my friend. Each heavy jet left me panting and quivering. Seiichi cried out and we lowered our gaze to watch through half-open eyes as his cock twitched, thin spurts of cream jetting out to cover the white of his belly fur.

The smell was so intense, so heavy, so erotic as I drew it in through gasping breaths.

I took a step backwards and my cock followed. When it pulled free with a plop, a heavy dollop of cum followed it, quickly staining the arm of the recliner. Seiichi raised his head and laughed before falling off the chair to the floor.

Exhaustion pulled at me, drawing me to crouch, and then lay on the floor.

All I wanted to do was sleep… Vashruc moaned in my head and I felt his control slipping. Lethargy drenched me, pulling me downwards. I just wanted to sleep, nothing more, nothing less. Seiichi was draped over my chest, his breathing not quite deep enough to be sleep, but close.

"Seiichi," I whispered, the transformed muzzle mine to control finally. "Are you okay?"

The fox's muzzle turned to me, his tongue hanging out. He blinked at me slowly, his pupils almost round. "That was amazing. Oh my God, I needed that." A paw reached out to brush against the side of my muzzle, caressing it with the gentlest of touches. "You are a god."

I rolled my eyes. "Are you okay, Seiichi?"

"Better than okay, I am fantastic." He murmured, continuing to caress my muzzle before sliding his paw down my massive chest, tracing a circle around my nipple. The sensation was sharp, almost painfully so, yet I still felt things stirring in me.

"Stop that, you'll wake him again," I hissed.

Seiichi grinned at me, his ears perking. "Oh?"

Before his paw could trace another circle, I grabbed it. He pulled against me, but the arm was stronger than I had thought. He giggled playfully. I growled back. "This isn't a game, Seiichi! My body is a monster!"

"Mm, but my kind of monster." The fox laughed and my ears went back, lips pulling back from the multitude of fangs in my mouth. Rage rolled through me like a thunderstorm. From somewhere in the back of my mind Vashruc gave a sated chuckle. My hand wrapped around my friend's throat and it took everything in my power not to squeeze.

Seiichi's ears splayed, the smile gone in an instant. Fear rose from him in waves, the scent sharp and biting to my nose and tongue. I lifted him off me and placed my nose almost to his. "I have a demon in my body. It has turned me into a freak. I need your help!"

He nodded slowly. "I... I might have something in one of my books."

I let go of him and he fell back to the floor, immediately crab-walking away from me. I wanted to immediately apologize, but the rage continued rolling in me. I wanted to grab him and break him. It was all I could do to relax my posture and my face, make myself less threatening. Seiichi yipped and darted to his bookshelf.

My gaze lingered on the sway of his tail and the tightness of his bum. I had never considered Seiichi as a sexual object, his orientation being so different than mine. But now, through new eyes, I could see how attractive he was. His form was slender and feminine, oddly more akin to what I looked for in a female partner. I wondered if I was a girl again, would I now find him attractive?

A small stack of books dropped beside him as he pulled them from the bookshelf. Sitting down, he pushed his tail to the side and was immediately flipping through pages. I crossed my legs on the floor and watched him, my elbows resting on my knees, my chin in my paws. He was cute. Really cute.

A deep chuckle rolled in the back of my head. *Do you see now why I was so eager to meet your friend?*

I had to admit, I did. *I am surprised you are so calm* Vashruc, *while he looks for a way to free me from you.*

You won't. You invited me into your body, you are stuck with me now. This isn't some movie where a couple of priests can remove me with a few outdated words and gestures. I am as much a part of you as your very soul is.

We will see, Vashruc, *we will see.* I was amazed at how quickly Seiichi bookmarked sections of text, often flitting between different volumes. I had never been like that in school and hated essays and anything to do with research because of it. But my friend moved with a grace that was almost fun to watch.

Your faith in your friend is admirable, but greater sorcerers than him have tried.

"Ahah, I think I have it!" Seiichi shouted, leaping to his feet, a book in his paw. He came over, his tail a rapid flash behind him. "So, I did some cross checking, and it looks like with the stuff I have here, I can change you back into yourself."

I nodded, the demon laughed. "That's a start."

Seiichi glanced up from the book and took a step back once he realized how close to me he was. The sway of his tail slowed. The scent of fear hit the air like a spike. I sighed. "Seiichi... I'm sorry. I know you really enjoyed yourself." I scratched my shin with my opposite foot. "I did too. But... look at me. Really look at me!"

The fox's gaze roamed over me and I could see a bit of pink appearing at the tip of his sheath.

"This isn't me; this isn't my body. I don't have full control of it and that scares me." I met his gaze. "I know you liked what he did to you, but you might not like the next thing, or the thing after that. And what if it's someone other than you? What if it's a little boy or girl? I need you to help me. I am sorry I scared you, but you weren't listening to me."

Seiichi sighed, ears splaying. "You're right. Damn it Kaiya, you're right. I was an idiot. Sorry."

Aww, so cute. Maybe I will make him beg for forgiveness next time I take him.

Shut up!

You're not done with me yet, child.

I looked at Seiichi. "You said you have a way of getting rid of this thing?"

"Well," Seiichi looked at the marked page in his book and then back to me. "Yes and no."

Vashruc's laughter tore through my mind.

"I can cast a spell that will reverse the transformation, but there's a catch."

My ears lowered. "Isn't there always? What is it? Slaying Slenderdude? Collecting the dew from an alien? Kissing a frog?"

"You, umm," the fox's tail curled against his leg. "You have to have sex with yourself."

"That's hardly something new. I masturbate all the time."

He met my gaze, his ears lowered and his tail practically merging with his leg. "No, you don't get it. You have to have sex with the demon, in the demon form."

Vashruc's laughter was constant now, loud enough to create stars behind my eyes. *What's a matter little one, don't think you're up for it?* The heavy member between my legs gave a twitch and my stomach flip-flopped. As if to accent his threat, the Vashruc reached down and cradled himself, his paws sliding up and down his sheath, drawing the top out. Seiichi whimpered in his throat, his eyes dropping to the slow glide of my paw over the hardening flesh.

Pain wracked my mind while I tore Vashruc's control away from my body. My paws moved away from my shaft, clenching into fists at my side. Gritting my teeth, ears flat against my head, I closed my eyes against the surge of the demon against my hold.

"Seiichi, whatever you need to do, do it fast."

The fox made a noise and I heard him scampering around the room. Images started to bombard my mind's eye. Men and women of various ages engaged in a number of sexual embraces, each as bizarre as the next. Warmth spread up my flattened ears and I could feel my body's member twitching at its full length. I wanted to touch it, badly.

A heady lid slammed shut and Seiichi cursed. I opened an eye as far as I dared to see that he had thrown on a pair of khakis and a tank top. He had a backpack beside where he stood and he was tossing things into it. Candles, plastic containers, black lacquered bowls, item after item went into it before he zipped it shut and looked at me. To his credit, his gaze met my open eye rather than stopping on the engorged beast pointing at him with unhidden lust.

"We need to go back to your place."

"Like this?" I motioned to my massive erection with both paws.

"Can you not point to it, please?" Seiichi bolted past me to his front closet. Throwing it open, he grabbed something and tossed it over me. Instinctively I pulled it around me. "This was a Rotti's I dated for a few weeks. He had told me he was a super dom."

"Not even close?"

"Not even close."

Vashruc tore my control away for a heartbeat. "Not like me?" He bared our teeth, his tail moving behind us.

Seiichi swallowed and turned, fumbling with the locks on his door. "We need to get to your house. I can smell his arousal and I really, *really* want another round. I haven't had sex like that since... ever."

Snarling I wrestled back control and moved past my friend and out into the early morning air. There was a strong breeze and inwardly I was thankful. I smelled heavily of sex and musk, so at least that would help. Now if I could only get rid of the giant tent in the front of the trench coat I was wearing, we'd be good, at least for now. At least my house was close, and there weren't a lot of people out and about yet.

This will never work.

"That's what you think."

Let me fuck the little fox again, over there at that playground. Such fun things can be done with a seesaw. The image flashed into my mind and I stumbled, my paw going out to a lamp post to steady myself. *Such delectable things...*

"Seiichi, we need to hurry, I don't know how much longer I will be able to keep this up."

The vulpine grabbed my oversized paw and pulled me along. My heart was hammering in my chest and I was having problems breathing. I barely dodged out of the way of a car as Seiichi yanked me through a crosswalk. I glanced back to see the young female hokkaido behind the wheel staring at me wide-eyed. Vashruc's purr rippled through me.

Shutting my eyes, I trusted my friend to guide me. *Why won't you just let me go!*

You already know the answer to that. I have not tasted the physical realm for decades, and I have cravings I must sate. You have no understanding of the pleasures of the flesh, nor does even your pet sorcerer. No, you wanted to know how to please your mate and I am giving that to you, little one. Am I not generous?

My mental retort froze. Images of my time with Sophia shot through my mind and I winced. I don't know if it was my own memory or the Vashruc's doing. Neither would have lessened the sting of it. I swore instead.

"Did you say something?" Seiichi glanced over his shoulder, ears raised.

"No," I said, without opening my eyes. "Are we almost there?" I hated how desperate I sounded.

"Yes. Do you have your keys?"

I opened the trench coat to reveal my nudity to him. Thankfully the erection had lowered, if only slightly. "Does it look like I have my keys?"

Seiichi swore before fishing in his khaki's pockets, coming up a moment later with a copied key. "Good thing you gave me this all those years ago isn't it?"

I groaned at the memory. It had been during a very, very desperate time in my life when I had just wanted another physical body close to me, sexually attractive to me or not.

My door swung inwards and I was the first inside. The air smelled like rotten orange juice and spilled cola, from the change I think. "It doesn't normally smell like this," I said more to myself than Seiichi. "Where do you need me?"

"In my—sorry, sorry. Old habit. Can you move your kotatsu out of the way?"

I grabbed the table and lifted, amazed at how little it weighed to me. Maybe I could get used to this. Maybe. Seiichi walked past me, pulling items out of his backpack. The lacquered bowls went down in a square, each carefully placed in relation to what I assumed was a compass he held balanced in the paw he also held the backpack's straps in. Next he set the pack down and sprinkled dashes of herbs into each bowl. I watched him from one corner of the room, afraid to speak or move, lest the demon see that as another opening to take control.

"Move there," the fox said, pointing to the center of the four bowls. I followed his finger and as soon as I was centered he touched a match to the herbs in the bowl nearest to him.

A jolt ran from the top of my ears to the soles of my feet paws as the other three bowls flared to life, curls of thick white smoke reaching towards the ceiling. Something inside me stretched and the tight feel of the demon wrapped around me loosened for the first time. Suddenly, it was easier to control the body.

"Better?" Seiichi asked, glancing up. I nodded and he smiled. Sitting cross-legged, he pulled the thickest of his books into his lap and started to read. The language was rough, sandpaper across your tongue rough. It coated me like a nest of serpents. My ears were flat enough to hurt, my tail against my legs. Even the ever seemingly present erection was nothing but a deflated sock beneath the coat.

How's it going? I inwardly sneered at Vashruc.

This will not work.

Seiichi traced something in the air and a bell tolled somewhere in the distance. I grunted as another jolt went through me, my breath frosting the air before my muzzle. The demon pushed and my body shed the trench coat to pool at my feet. A paw went to my member, tracing the sheath with a finger. Seiichi looked up, stumbled on a word.

The air lost some of its heaviness and Vashruc grabbed the shaft, slowly rolling its paw back and forth, bringing it forth from its sheath. The fox recovered, the next few words out of his muzzle louder, his ears flicking forwards and back. I pushed against the demon and tore my paw away from its teasing. There was a hiss as Seiichi turned a page and the world seemed to hold its breath.

His next words had me doubled up on the floor, clawing at my stomach as I retched what felt like my very soul out of my transformed body. The fluid was heavy and thick strings of it clung to my muzzle and chest. Seiichi continued his reading, his ears perked towards the tome when I looked at him, pleading crying out from my gaze.

Another page turned, and I was on all fours, heaving out my existence. A tiny part of me wondered if the stain would come out of the flooring, or if the vixen downstairs would notice. Vashruc raged within me, invisible claws raking the inside of my mind even as I felt his grip on me lessening.

With a final wrack of my body, I felt the demon slip out of me and into the mass soaking into my floorboards. I laughed and looked up at my vulpine friend.

You aren't done with me yet, little one!

My eyes dropped to the mass as it quivered and slowly rose from the floor. I snarled at it, baring my fangs. Outside his square of bowls, I saw Seiichi watching, the book set aside, his gaze on the shaping form between us.

Slowly it turned on itself, spiralling upwards, features forming as it seemed to settle. Ears flicked upwards as fur sprouted from the goo, the body solidifying with each new change. My muzzle fell open as familiar eyes blinked and stared at me, the muzzle splitting in a smile I only saw in photos or the mirror. Dainty paws travelled down the front of the body, one I often considered too pudgy, to caress between its inner thighs.

"I told you we aren't done yet," the copy of me said with Vashruc's voice. "And though this is just a copy of you, I must say, it feels like the real thing." It let out a moan while it pinched both of its nipples, drawing them to rosy peaks.

I growled, the hairs along my back prickling as they rose. My front paws dug their claws into the wood of the floor, catching on the seams between the boards. "Get the hell out of my house!"

The copy of me laughed. "I doubt it." He motioned at Seiichi with his thumb. "His magic is what's keeping us separated and me here. I honestly am surprised; I didn't think sorcerers of his power still existed in this plane."

I thought I saw Seiichi's tail give a short wagging swish behind him. If the demon heard it, he didn't react.

"You can not get rid of me, the sorcerer himself said as much. The best we can do is an… agreement."

I hadn't forgotten.

I hit him like a ton of bricks, my body slamming him to the ground, my teeth locked around the imitation of my body's throat. I could smell myself, so familiar, yet alien to my altered body's nose. Vashruc laughed while I pinned him, my left paw easily holding him down by his throat. He grinned up at me.

He licked his muzzle. "I knew you had it—"

My right paw came across his muzzle in a backhand. It wasn't as hard as I wanted to hit him, but it was enough to turn his head. His laughter grew while he turned his face to look at me again. His grin widened.

That earned Vashruc another slap.

His smile was still there when he looked at me again, only this time there was something more there. Something that brought a heat to my chest. I could feel my altered body getting aroused. Another slap, and the look the demon gave me from my eyes made me sit back, bringing him with me as I raised my paw.

"Oh what sweet pain." He coughed with a wince, "How I have missed you. You know, you'd make an excellent demon, Kaiya."

A growl rumbled in my chest. Delicate paws grasped my forearm as he tried to pull back. I wasn't squeezing, but the position he was in, half-way between standing and squatting, looked uncomfortable. I let the copy of my body hang there for a moment before shoving Vashruc to the hardwood face-first with a snarl. His ass was in the air and I admired it. It wasn't often I got to see such a nice view of my own rear. It was nice and round, perhaps not as firm as I wanted it, but it had a nice shape to it.

While I held Vashruc down using his scruff, I used my free paw to caress the presented ass. It felt surreal to be touching my own body, but my altered form approved, my member now fully out of its sheath, jumping with my heart beat. My paw continued to drag through the fur on the demon's rear, tracing each angle of it, teasing the crease between cheeks.

"No wonder Sophia got bored with your sex life. Your foreplay is terribly boring."

My first slap caught both of us by surprise. I hadn't intended to, but the meaty thwack made me grin at Vashruc's gasp. I rubbed the spot I had slapped, tracing the tender flesh under the fur before drawing my paw back.

The demon moaned at the second slap. The sound of my flesh hitting his echoed in the room. I heard a second gasp and glanced up to see Seiichi watching us with rapt attention, the fly of his khaki's open, his shaft peeking through while he teased it. I grinned at him and slapped my body double again, drawing forth another gasp and moan.

Rubbing the spot, I gripped the cheek tight, my claws digging into the tender skin, making the demon squirm, legs parting slightly to reveal the treasure within.

I had always been curious what my pussy looked like without using a mirror. Sure, girlfriends had told me that it was pretty with its smaller outer lips. One girl had even called it a cute little present wrapped up in the neatest of bows. But now, the sight of my own sex, the scent of it rolling off across my muzzle, brought a rumble to my chest. Under me my member throbbed, and it took all of my willpower not to drive its length into that slit. I didn't know if the damage I did to this form would transfer back when I merged with Vashruc, so I wasn't taking any chances.

Instead, I ran a finger along the slit, drawing dew forth on the tip of my claw. My doppelganger shivered in my grip, whimpering as he bit his lip. I found his entrance and slowly ran my finger around it before sliding it in. He was wet of course, it *was* my body and I knew it well. Vashruc growled lightly and I shoved my finger in, cutting it off and turning it into a long moan.

"Sophia would probably be... ugh... asleep by now at this—"

My thumb pressed against his clit, cutting him off. I held it there, rolling it under the pad until it looked like he was too busy panting to speak. Raising my thumb, I let my finger slide as far inwards as it could while I felt familiar walls tense against me. When I went as far as I dared, I eased the finger out almost to my claw before shoving it in again. The demon wiggled beneath my paw, tongue starting to peek from behind his muzzle. Grinning, I picked up the pace as I slid my finger in and out of him, teasing his inner walls while I did.

He cried out when a second finger joined the first, only this time I didn't play gentle. Something in me was pushing against me to take him, to shove the throbbing mass between my legs into his tight pussy and fuck the hell out of Vashruc. The thought of it drew my mind back slightly, but not nearly enough to stop my actions, or to kill the desire that was burning within me. I had to do this, and weirdly enough, I wanted to as well.

"Just fuck me already!" Vashruc snarled, glancing back at me, the bangs of his hair hiding all but a sliver of his eye. I grinned in returned, wagging a finger on my free paw.

I shifted my body and started to slide my fingers in and out of the demon's form in swift motions. He reached out, his claws digging into my wooden floor as if trying to get away. This only made me pump my arm faster, turning my wrist this way and that, bending the fingers slightly at the odd moment to draw out his moans and cries. His scent was heavy in the air now, mixing with mine, Seiichi's own scent lingering like an aftertaste at the back of each breath.

"Not so coy now, are we demon?" I snarled as I shifted my paw and pressed my fingertips against the fleshy mass just inside Vashruc's entrance and to the front. My thumb pressed against his clit and with a simple roll of it the creature screamed out. Knees, thighs, and inner walls clenched together as his body was rocked with wave after wave. I grinned to myself while I kept up the pressure of my fingers, making sure to draw it out as long as possible.

"You think this will break me little one?" The demon whispered, his body quivering under my caress. "I have…umf…I have experienced pleasure that would make angels weep!"

I drew my fingers from his slick passage in one swift motion, his fluids arching through the air in a thin, glittering rainbow. Releasing his neck, I stood, member proud, a thick pearl of pre shining at its tip. "Is that so?" I couldn't help but grin, flashing my teeth. Looking over, I saw Seiichi still holding himself, which impressed me. My body felt tight around my groin, my member bouncing slightly with my heartbeat. I wanted to take my possessed body badly, but somehow Vashruc had kept back from the cliff of orgasm.

"You need to finish it," Seiichi said, voice deep, almost sultry. His gaze moved to where my body lay on the floor, ass still in the air, arousal darkening the fur around the flushed lips of his sex. I nodded at my friend and walked over to my body, careful to avoid the slick floor where my pre had dripped, as well as the growing pool under the demon's slit.

Reaching down, I grabbed Vashruc by his throat, raising him up onto shaking legs. I leaned in beside his ear where it splayed out. "Let's end this."

The demon made a noise in its throat as he thrashed against me, but I didn't care. I only cared that his passage was soaked and my member was aching for release. With a paw back on the scruff of his neck, I shoved him against the air between two of the bowls. I was rewarded with a solid thud as Vashruc's body hit the wall, splaying him against a shimmering barrier. On the other side Seiichi crab-walked back until he hit the wall of my apartment, his paw never leaving his member.

I kicked the demon's legs apart, and with my free hand guided my member between the cleft of my doppelganger's ass cheeks. I played it up and down the cleft before dipping lower, the mushroom head of my cock running down his slit to rub against his clit. As he moaned, I slid my length against the tiny bud, each vein plucking against it before sliding back and pressing my tip against his entrance.

"About fucking time!" Vashruc gasped.

Squeezing the paw around his scruff, I pushed myself forward, his slick passage resisting against the sheer size of my head before it popped in. "Fuck!" The demon struggled, ears splayed. He kicked back at me, tried to claw at my forearms, but I pulled back on his scruff, pulling his head back while I shoved my shaft deeper. Each inch it moved felt like heaven, each bump of his inner walls a caress of pure sensation. With every inch that slid inwards, Vashruc tore at the barrier, claws unable to find purchase in the shimmering wall.

With a grunt, I hit resistance. Looking down I was surprised to see that the copy of my body was taking just over three quarters of my shaft, less than Seiichi had. Perhaps his collection of dildos was for more than show. My gaze moved upwards, admiring how the demon's slit hugged the pulsing length of my shaft, his body seeming to be held up by just it and my one paw.

Vashruc panted for a moment before letting out a grunt. "Poor little one isn't enough of a slut to take it all is she?"

I didn't give him an answer, instead pulling back a couple of inches and then pushed inwards, my tip bumping against his innermost depths. He cried out, all four paws scrambling against the barrier now, his muzzle open in a cry of pleasure and pain. It made me pull his head back further as I started to slide myself in and out of him in ever quickening thrusts. Vashruc's cries rose in volume, eyes flashing between opened and closed with each shove into his tight body.

My free paw wrapped around Vashruc's muzzle, pulling his head back to the limit of his body's ability as I started to hammer against him. He thrashed, moans and cries rocking off the walls of my apartment. Somewhere I could hear a thumping coming from my downstairs neighbor, but I ignored it, instead moving my hips faster and faster. Each thrust pounded Vashruc upwards, and judging from the look Seiichi was giving the stolen form, he could see my member pressing outwards from within the doppelganger's body.

The thought of that brought me to the edge.

I roared before clamping my jaws on the back of the false me's neck. My member pulsed and I felt my cum surge from me in rolling jets deep within Vashruc's womb. He screamed out, his body shaking as his inner walls pushed back against the fleshy intruder, milking as much of my seed as it could. From the edge of my hearing Seiichi's cry joined ours while I poured everything into the demon. Then, with one final burst of cum, I brought my forehead to the back of his head and my world went black.

***

I awoke to my body aching both inside and out. I rolled to my side, the effort of it making me groan. Opening my eyes, I saw Seiichi sweeping up bits of broken lacquered bowls.

"When did that happen?" I managed to ask, slowly pushing myself up so I was on all fours. I felt like I had been split in half, and as I moved, something oozed from between my slit to plop heavily onto the wood floor.

Seiichi zipped his backpack up. "I think it was when you climaxed. I'm not sure; I was kind of... indisposed."

I glanced around. My floor looked like a game show studio; a mess of milky and clear fluids covered so much of it. I would have to spend the next week trying to clean it out. The air stank like sex. I would have to spray everything down with diluted vodka to get rid of the smell as well as the germs. So many germs.

Moving slowly, I managed to sit my tender bum on the floor well away from the pool of various fluids. "So, where's the demon?"

Seiichi tossed his backpack over one shoulder. "According to the tome, you absorbed him." Crouching in front of me, he tapped my chest. "He's in there somewhere."

We stared at each other for a long moment. My heart was hammering in my tightening chest. Panic surged in me, my breath getting shorter. Vashruc *was in me? No, no, no...*

My ears lowered and Seiichi leaned in and kissed me. It wasn't like the forceful kiss between him and the demon body, but rather a dainty thing. Something pushed me and I slid my tongue past his lips and caressed his before pulling back. He smiled as he tilted his head to the side. "That's what I thought."

I tilted my head to the side in a mirror of him. "What?"

Standing, he helped me get to my feet and motioned towards a mirror in the corner of the room. I stood before it and looked back at him through the reflection. "Yeah, awesome. Naked me looking like I've been gangbanged by both a football and a roller derby team at the same time. So, what of it?"

He came up behind me, running his paws over my chest and sides. The urge to shove him down and take him surged in me, and while I watched, my eyes took on a reddish glow and my body started to enlarge. Seiichi took a step back while I closed my eyes and counted to ten. When I opened them I was plain little me.

"See what I mean?" He asked, smiling. "I think with time you will be able to control the transformation better. Just watch those urges, they could get you into some pretty weird situations if you let them loose."

"But it will take practice…" My ears perked and I couldn't help but laugh and smile at him.

His own smile broke upon his muzzle and his tail wagged behind him. "Lots and lots of practice I hope. With me specifically, if you don't mind?"

I stepped towards him and grabbed his scruff, pulling him into me for a deeper, longer kiss. When we finally broke, I licked the top of his nose. "Sounds like a plan. But until then, I need to clean up."

He chuckled as I lead him to the door and we said our good-byes. Turning to the apartment I let out a sigh as my gaze fell on the vixen figure. It lay on the floor, knocked over during some part of the evening. Running my paw through my tangled hair, I went over and picked it up. This was going back into its box as soon as possible. *Then* I could shower…

***

It was two weeks before I had the nerve to call Sophia. That said, she hadn't really made any attempt to call or text me. When I finally got through to her, she still sounded pissed.

"What do you want?" Her tone was sharp enough to make my ears lower slightly.

"I have something to show you," I said, taking a deep breath. "I think I finally get what you wanted that night with the video. We should have talked. About what we like in sex and what we both wanted before it got out of control. But I get it now."

"Oh?" I could hear her foot thumping the floor of her room over the phone. "What changed your mind?"

"I kind of had a life changing event."

"What kind of event?"

I couldn't help myself from grinning, even though she couldn't see it. "You will just have to come over and find out. Just be prepared for a *big* surprise and possibly the best night of your life, okay?"

The beat of her foot stopped. "You're right, we should have talked. I should have said something… I'll be there in ten." I could hear her smile even over the phone. "This better be good, and you're right, maybe we should." She hung up.

"Oh it will be," I said to the dead line. Laughing, I faced the front door and let my imagination run wild, a warm crawling sensation rippled across my body as I started to change. "It will be…"

Bill Kieffer

Bill Kieffer is also known as Greyflank, the Typing Horse. He is a member of the Transformation Story Archive Mailing list so just about everything about him is subject to change. He needs to get out more. He lived under his bed for about a decade, so he's got a lot of time to make up for.

He's written everything from comic books to porn to interviews. His short stories have recently appeared in *ROAR 7*, *ROAR 8*, B*leak Horizons*, I*nhuman Acts*, *Seven Deadly Sins*, and *A Century of Anthropomorphics* (featuring his first Ursa Major Award nominated short story, *The Good Sport*). Recently released: *Cold Blood: Fatal Fables* from Jaffa Books is a collection of noir stories that take place on Aesop's World. The story in this collection is set in either that world's future or that world's past. You decide.

Bill Kieffer appears at least once a month with a publisher's interview or book review over at UndergroundBookReviews.Org

Franklin Leo

Franklin Leo is a writer and academic currently living in Orlando, Florida. Her work has typically focused on posthuman theory, the horror genre, and romance between many types of creatures, even fictional ones.

She may be found discussing and blogging her life on Twitter at Fictionfelid, where posts on cats and general topics take up her time.

Friday Donnelly

Friday is a transformation-minded otter who currently lives near Boston, MA. Ever since watching Disney's Brother Bear approximately a thousand times (much to his parent's annoyance), the idea of becoming something different than what he is and seeing the world through new eyes has appealed to him. Whether exploring what it'd be like to reside in a different person's body or exploring further up the tree of life, he's always restless for a new view on the world. He explores this hunger in his stories and writing.

This is his first dip into transformation in anthology format, but he has a novel exploring these themes on the chopping block currently. At some point in the future he hopes to serve it up to an eager audience.

Online it's easiest to find his work at his Furaffinity page 'Dandin' and his personal media presence on Twitter @Friday_Otter.

Tarl "Voice" Hoch

Tarl is a horror and erotica writer who also dabbles in other genres. When not writing, he can be found being a host on Fangs And Fonts, playing in the snow, or entertaining his cats.

A list of his works can be found on Goodreads: https://www.goodreads.com/author/show/5759304.Tarl_Voice_Hoch

ABOUT THE ARTIST

Sabretoothed Ermine

Sabretoothed Ermine is a Canadian artist who has been doing "furry" art full-time since 2009 and, despite what people may say about turning a hobby into a career, still loves it. Though she hasn't attended any art schools (that would mean moving to a city, ugh!) she has been drawing since she could hold a pencil, and anthropomorphic animals have always been her subject of choice. You may see her at a convention now and again, but like most weasels she's generally pretty reclusive and happy to stay with her husband in their beautiful forested homeland of British Columbia.

All of her furry art and her current commission info can be found in her FurAffinity gallery at: *furaffinity.net/user/sabretoothedermine/*

Or if you just want to say hi, feel free to email her at: *ermine@ermineart.com*

www.ingramcontent.com/pod-product-compliance
Lightning Source LLC
Chambersburg PA
CBHW071321130626
46556CB00004B/1697